IN THE SHADOW OF THE PAST

A Prague Crime Novel

P A WILSON

Ebook ISBN: 978-1-927669-52-5
Paperback ISBN: 978-1-927669-53-2
Audio book ISBN:978-1-927669-54-9

Free book

Claim your copy of Buying Into Death when you sign up
for my newsletter and follow Charity as she solves her
fastest case yet!

Chapter 1

It was my first vacation in something like five years. At least that's what people back at the office thought. For me it wasn't just a fun trip to Prague. I'd made some shady decisions in my work, but the last one scared me. At thirty-five, I thought I knew myself. It came as a huge surprise to find I was capable of that much violence.

So, here I sat, looking for a way out. A new life. If no one at home found out how far past my personal lines I went, then I had time, but I couldn't count on the secret staying quiet for long.

For this week I had two priorities. One, to find a place where I could start again with a new identity, in a country house that I could rent out for retreats or whatever. A place I could hide away like a hermit for a while. The other priority was money. Living cost less here, part of why I chose the Czech Republic, and because my grandmother came from here. My dad named me Sharka after her. I looked almost exactly like her in the few pictures she had kept from her youth. I thought it time someone from the family came back.

When the seat belt sign pinged off after landing, everyone but me rushed to turn on their phones and check in with the world. I treasured the last few minutes of peace and disconnection. But now I needed something to do other than stare out at the passing view of buildings and the barriers between the highway and the surrounding scenery. As soon as the phone found a network, it chimed with a message to remind me my roaming plan was active and then welcomed me to the local network. I planned to take advantage of the fact I had a generous data plan thanks to the law firm where I worked as an investigator. My phone, their plan, a great deal and all the privacy I needed — until I ditched my past life permanently.

I had a list of missed calls from Jack Hennessy, one of the partners at the firm. Had my luck failed already? I ignored the notifications. If they'd found out and called the cops, then I would just enjoy my time and face the consequences when I got dragged back. I hated the job anyway, so if they fired me, I wouldn't mind so much. If the police came after me in Prague, a charge of grievous bodily harm would seriously delay my plans. And with the right pressure, someone would call the locals. Jack exerted pressure all day, expertly and liberally.

I turned my phone off and closed my eyes. Jet lag was hitting hard. On top of the nine-hour difference, the last time my head hit a pillow was thirty hours ago thanks to last minute details on a few cases.

The taxi pulled up to my hotel. Just a few blocks from the tourist points but still in a quiet area. Small shops and a couple of restaurants populated both sides of the narrow street. It was warm in the afternoon sun, and quiet. I might get comfortable with the lack of honking and yelling.

The driver took my bags to the lobby and I paid him

and gave him a tip. Checking in was quick; I guess they were used to tired visitors looking forward to their bed and a long nap.

OF COURSE, now that I could lay on a bed, my brain craved some entertainment. Between jet lag and now a little guilt at not returning a call that might or might not be the precursor to a jail sentence, I couldn't rest. I'd unpacked, and even ironed the few items that needed it. The busy work made me realize how little I had prepared for leaving everything behind. Amassing a load of clothes was never my style, but I should have paid for a second case. My plan hadn't been in the forefront of my thoughts when I packed for a vacation, not an escape. I had a lot of shopping in my future.

The room was small with no balcony, so I couldn't burn off the restlessness by pacing. Even with the time difference, dinner wouldn't be in the next hour. But I was in a new city and possibly my new home. It would do me some good to go out and find my way around.

I grabbed my jacket and phone; the jeans and tee-shirt I wore on the plane would be fine for a stroll. I had an app that would give me a route to walk, maybe end with an early dinner and then I could sleep. It didn't feel like a vacation yet. Exhaustion kind of disconnected me from everything. I hoped that would change tomorrow because I didn't have the time to lay around recovering.

My phone rang: Jack.

I went cold. Why was he so intent on talking to me? To tell me I was fired and dodging an arrest warrant? His hands weren't clean in the situation that sent me on the run. The thought didn't give me much reassurance since he was a lawyer and I couldn't recognize a tort from a contract dispute. I tapped to ignore. I'm a coward.

It rang again. This time I accepted the call because I couldn't count on him to give up. And if I had to face the consequences, I needed to know now. "I'm on vacation."

"It's too early in the morning for me to argue," Jack said in his court voice.

I felt my body go off fight or flight. When he used the court voice, it meant he was going to persuade me to do something. Hopefully he had no plans to ask me to turn myself in or keep me around until the cops came. I tensed again.

"Fine, what is it?"

"I need your help," he said.

Just like the last time, and would I be in worse trouble after? "I'm not in Vancouver."

"I'm aware. I need help in Prague."

I didn't believe in coincidences. No one knew where I'd gone, only that I was on vacation. Jack thought he could put me on a short rein, but I would find out who told him where I was and cut that particular leash. "So, what does that have to do with me?"

"Don't try to lie. I found you there and I can find you again if you move on," he said. "I have friends who can locate any information I want. And will do what I ask without arguing."

I don't know if he meant it to be menacing, but it kind of came off as braggy. "Then they can help you," I said. "I haven't taken any time off in years, Jack." I hoped the whine in my voice didn't sound quite so pathetic in his ears.

"It won't take long. It's not something I can get just anyone to do. I need someone I can trust."

"Did you need help before you found out I was here?"

My exhaustion helped me to sound like the bitch I felt, something I usually kept under control. If I'd gone to Hawaii, would he have needed help there? Now that I asked myself that, I realized the answer was yes. Jack had global interests, and some of them were a little shady, and I guessed some of them were more than a little. I could keep arguing or I could get it over with. Knowing what he wanted might help me turn him down. "What do you want?"

"Just listen," he said.

I couldn't believe he spoke to me like an employee. I had never been an employee, always a consultant, and we'd both insisted on keeping our relationship clear. But if I didn't let him get to the point, he would never let me say no and carry on with my holiday. I sat on the bed, careful not to lay down and give in to the inevitable drag of sleeplessness. "Go ahead."

Jack didn't speak for a moment. I heard him cough, as though trying to control his emotions. That got my attention more than any comment about my abilities. Jack didn't show emotion.

"My daughter, Rio. You met her once."

He expected a response and I was in no mood to linger over the conversation. What good would a power move like that do?

"I remember her." Whatever it took to keep him talking and no more. I did recall meeting her though, at a firm celebration. She'd been a very precocious fourteen. The way she pretended to know everything annoyed the hell out of me — until I found out she was about to enter university. Amazing how knowing she did know everything made her less annoying and far more interesting.

"She went to university in Prague," he said. "A private

institution. Data analysis of some sort. I wanted her to stay home, go to UBC."

Another pause. But this time I had nothing to say. My brain wondered why he sent a fourteen-year-old to a foreign country. And then it caught up and I realized Rio would be almost seventeen by now.

He cleared his throat again. "She's been kidnapped."

Chapter 2

That made me sit up. I'd expected some trouble; a run-in with the cops, maybe a little too much underage partying; maybe a favor to pay her bail. But it made no sense now that I thought it through. Jack had plenty of legal contacts all over the world. He didn't need me for simple things like bail.

No matter how intelligent she was, kidnapped teenagers needed help. She was barely seventeen, and she must be terrified. I might want to say no to Jack because he was a bully and an ass, but I had better reasons. I was not the right person to do this. Rio needed an expert and I lacked that, even at home. "I don't have any connections here."

"You can find connections. You're good at using people. You always have been. That's one of the reasons why you're so valuable to the firm. Did you have all your connections when you started?"

Probably not ones valuable enough to his firm to make up for what I did, but it seemed they hadn't found out yet. "It took a long time for me to find people I could trust. We don't have years." I tried another tack. "Tell me what happened?"

"I got a call. They want money. She's still alive."

"Is that all?"

"It's the core of the call."

"You should go to the police," I said. Avoiding the authorities in these situations might be a knee-jerk reaction. Their success rate couldn't be all that high when it came to kidnappings on a different continent. Too many links in the chain meant too many opportunities to screw up. I still had to try. "They'll reach out to Interpol, it's the best way to deal with this."

"I want you to do this," Jack said. "Keep it quiet and bring her back. The cops won't be able to do what you do."

The silence felt heavy and I started to doubt I got away with the last case. But it was still silence. I refused to give him the satisfaction of voicing my fear.

"You know what I can do at home, where I'm surrounded by my contacts," I said. "You know I can get results in Vancouver, maybe not how, but you've never been interested in the details."

"I have ways of getting details. You can't be naive enough to think I relied on your reports."

"Not naive. It's my business what lines I cross."

"Not just your business. If you commit a crime for information on a case, the law firm is liable."

My heart beat faster. He knew. Jack would never come out and say it, but he knew.

"It could be true, even if I free Rio. If I have to break the law, you won't be able to get them convicted."

"You worry about getting her free. I'm not concerned about prison sentences."

"I haven't said yes," I pointed out. "If I did agree to

help, I'm in a different country, a different culture, and I'm not sure I can get in deep enough fast enough to save her."

"Will you try?"

"I don't think you want me to try, Jack. Trying is more likely to get her killed than rescued."

There was silence on the line. This time it had a different feel. It felt like he was making a decision. I couldn't say what made me think it, maybe I just hoped he was, because the only other option I could think of involved a short future for my dreams.

"I can't go to the cops because... There may be some things I don't want them looking at." The confession rattled out as though he was fighting every word. Jack didn't like projecting weakness, even when it came to family.

"You'd protect your shady business at the risk of your daughter's life?" I couldn't believe he would do that. I'm not saying he was a moral guy, but he must know the facts would eventually come out. His reputation in court wouldn't survive.

"Not just *my* shady dealings," he said.

So, he does know.

"I'll take my chances with the police." I controlled my gut reaction to fight him.

He laughed, a mean little sound. "I know you're bluffing. Let's get to the real point. I'll pay you whatever you ask. I'll keep your secret. I made sure no one else knows, so you can trust me."

I let him think it over. Maybe if I kept silent, he'd say something I could actually believe.

He filled the silence. "I'll give you whatever help you need." He was finally starting to sound like a dad desperate to save his daughter.

"If you want Rio back, you want the best people

looking for her. I can't believe that *I* am the best you can find." I got to my feet and started pacing; three steps forward, turn, three steps the other direction.

"In this situation, you are," he said. "I won't take your secret to the police if you don't agree. The people I tell will do you more damage than a prison term."

I didn't want to answer him. I knew what he meant, and I didn't know how to keep my fear hidden. Before this I had plans. Being here or being somewhere in Europe. Doing something different. I took a quiet breath and asked, "What's worse than prison?" I knew fear made people assume the worst and maybe I was wrong. If his threat was going to work, I needed him to say it.

"I'll spread the news to the family of the man Hopper killed." Hopper was the client I crossed the line for. All so he could dodge a murder charge. I guess now it was going all the way and helping someone get away with murder.

"So, he wasn't innocent after all." I tried to stall until I could think of another way to save Rio.

What Jack was threatening would send some brutal people after me. People who wouldn't stop looking until they found me, no matter how much I changed my life. No matter how far I moved to avoid detection. "You know what reporting me will mean," I said. "With the cops. I might get away with reasonable force. I mean, I'm just a woman and he's a big man with a violent history."

"A big man, with a violent history, and lots of friends exactly like him."

I still refused to believe he could convince me to help him. I believed I was the last person who would find Rio alive. And I didn't really believe Jack would do that, set a gang after me. He was elbow deep in this too. He had to know I would tell them about his part in everything that happened. He'd be punished and maybe worse than me.

"So, what's your answer? You're going to do this. The longer you delay, the worse it gets for Rio."

Chills crossed my neck at his words. He sounded more like one of the kidnappers than a concerned parent. I could only think of one other tactic Jack might consider.

Chapter 3

"Why don't you just pay the ransom?" And hope the kidnappers play fair.

"You mean why don't I want to pay, right? Like I think my daughter isn't worth all my money?"

Yes, that's exactly what I was thinking. "Look, I don't know what the problem is. You say you want Rio back, but you keep pushing to take the route least likely to succeed."

The silence bristled with anger. I heard his breathing and imagined the look in his eyes. Jack never took no easily. Part of the reason I was in this much trouble was because he always demanded answers and ignored problems. It's not an excuse, I could've said no to him before. I wasn't going to be so stupid this time.

When he finally spoke, it was quiet, menacing. "I can pay whatever they eventually ask for, but I have no guarantee they'll let her go. Even if they do, she's still in Prague, not at home."

"You wouldn't come here to take her home?" Shouldn't he have been on the first plane out? Although, if he were here, I couldn't hang up on him to get a pause to think.

And face-to-face I'd have no way to get out of the job. I counted the distance between us as a blessing, or at least an advantage.

"I can't. Don't ask why, just believe me," he said.

I've learned to take statements like 'believe me' and 'trust me' as signs to do the opposite when people said them. But this was Jack, not some criminal. And my gut said there must be a difference between asshole and criminal.

"I need someone on site," he said. "If I must pay a ransom, I'll need you to do the exchange. I want the names of these people and why they took my daughter."

Knowing Jack, I figured they wouldn't get to enjoy the money. "If I can't do it?"

I wasn't going to be a scapegoat and I couldn't ignore the fact this was a fight for my life as much as Rio's. There might be a chance I could disappear after hanging up. It wouldn't be clean, but I knew how to do it. Would I be able to live with Rio's death until someone found me and ended everything with a gun?

"Your secret is safe. That's all you're worried about, right?"

For the next few minutes I had the power position. I didn't believe Jack would accept that I tried my best unless he had Rio back and the names of her kidnappers. And even if he did, it would only last until he needed another bit of dirty business done. With enough money, I wouldn't care. It would buy me a new identity. No one would think Sharka Lewis would settle down in a villa and live a quiet life.

"First, you let me resign with no repercussions. I'm not coming back to the firm." If I could avoid it, I wouldn't go back to Vancouver. Getting involved in what was really a police case might force me back.

"That won't be hard to manage."

If he made me out to be shady, it would affect everyone I loved. "Without slaughtering my reputation."

"Don't worry, I won't jeopardize the cases you investigated."

That might come in handy in the future. If he put my secret out in the public, all the cases I touched would come into question. The thought eased a load of tension and I started to feel like I might actually survive this with my freedom intact.

How much should I ask for? It wasn't like I could submit an expense sheet. Any help I needed would come out of my fee, and help could be expensive. I had enough to start on my new life, but this was the opportunity to build a future.

"I want five hundred thousand. Half today, half when Rio is found, even if I don't find her in time." My stomach turned at the thought of getting paid for finding her body, but I had to take the advantage.

"In your personal account?" Jack didn't flinch. I should have asked for a full million.

"Yes." The money wouldn't be in that account long. I had hidden accounts, something I learned from the financial lawyers in the firm.

"One more thing," Jack said. "Check your phone."

My text notification binged. I opened it to see a picture of Rio. In a dim room that looked like a basement. She was tied to a chair. I saw the terror in her eyes. She looked like the kidnappers had given her a beating, but not enough to do permanent damage. She was alive. That counted for something.

"Did you set a tracker on the source?" If they could trace the text it would give me somewhere to start.

"No. Whoever they are, they know how to avoid a trace."

They also hadn't bothered to cover Rio's eyes. I hoped they were wearing masks, otherwise she wouldn't survive this. It bothered me to agree with him, but he was probably right not to hand over the money as a first tactic. If I couldn't get to her in time, all we'd find is a body, if we were lucky. If they believed Jack would pay, they'd keep trying. Of course, that logic relied on them asking for a ransom.

"I know what you think of me, Sharka." Jack's voice shook. "I need my daughter back alive. I need to you to tell me who they are and why they did this."

"And if I can only save Rio?"

"It will be good enough. I have other people who can get the rest."

I wanted time to think this through. I knew I couldn't say no outright. No matter how much of an asshole her father acted, Rio didn't deserve to die. If I was going to be drawn into this, I couldn't go blind. "I'll call you back." I ended the call before he could argue and put my phone on 'do not disturb'.

This was when I needed all my brain functions, and jet lag robbed me of that. I couldn't take a nap because my body thought it was morning. I picked up my phone and searched for the Czech word for No Doz. The crash would be horrendous when this ended, but I would deal with the consequences later. I headed for the closest pharmacy, breathing in the fresh air and enjoying being able to walk more than a few feet.

I WAS ONLY GONE for fifteen minutes. I didn't take the

pills because my mind still functioned okay, and I knew I would need the caffeine later.

I checked my account and saw Jack had transferred three hundred and fifty thousand dollars to it. I guess the extra was an incentive. I hoped it wasn't because he planned to take his money back, or renege on the final payment. Or make sure I needed it to defend myself in court.

None of those worries fell into the category of 'I can do something about it now', so I set the process in motion to move the payment to a hidden account. I tried not to think too much about where the funds came from; that amount couldn't come from the firm's account without questions. Even if the money had a little dirt on it, that would be gone by the time it hit the last bank.

Now that I had time to think, I realized there was no downside to taking this on. Jack already had the power to send someone to hurt me, if not kill me. If I said no to him, I would be just as battered and relatively poor. If I said yes and he betrayed me, at least the money could give me a chance to disappear before anyone found me. I turned the phone back to 'disturb'. To his credit, Jack only made two calls and three texts in the time it was off. I hit the button to return one of the calls; no way I would do this by text.

"Don't hang up on me again," Jack said by way of greeting.

"I had to think," I said. "I got the money."

"Bring Rio back and the names of her kidnappers and you'll get the same bonus at the end."

He really didn't know when to shut up. Every time he pushed, or offered more payment, I lost a little trust in him. "Tell me what they asked for." If I didn't take some control back right now, this would end up with me just following his useless orders. If this case had any chance of success, I needed to do this my way.

"They haven't asked for the ransom yet," he said. "They said to wait and be ready to pay when they contacted me again."

That was weird. "Kidnappers who don't want to get paid right away?" Jack had no reason to lie about it, but I still felt a huge ball of suspicion in my gut.

"I'm telling you what they said."

He was curt now. I guess he thought the persuasion stage was done now that he'd paid me. Maybe the kidnappers didn't want money. "Does she know something? Something worth more than cash? Something you wouldn't want to pay?"

"Rio isn't part of my business life," Jack said. "She doesn't know anything about that. And I *will* pay anything to have her back."

"Is it possible they think she knows something?" I wished I could see his face because something was missing, and I couldn't make my brain identify it. Maybe I was just reading things into his words and attitude, allowing my own fear to distort the message. But he'd been clear on the threat. "Jack, let me set up a video call."

"There's no time," he said.

The first time we agreed on something. I couldn't afford the time to argue about something that didn't really matter. "If not your business, is there something in your personal life these people can use as leverage?" It could be a criminal case; Jack defended people. Although, he has corporate clients... no, I've been watching too many conspiracy movies.

"I have no idea what they think, Sharka. I can't deny I stepped across the line a time or two, but I can't think of anything that would be worth taking my daughter. They'll want money. Believe me, this will be about getting paid."

I wasn't sure I believed him, but time was passing, and I needed to find a starting point. "Do you do any business in Prague?"

"No."

"Anyone you can introduce me to, someone who can help?"

"If I did, you would know." He told someone to come in. "I need to go. Let me know when you find something."

This time he ended the call.

Chapter 4

I wasn't finished with Jack and I couldn't let him control the flow of information. More importantly, I needed to set the boundaries if we were going to find Rio before they killed her. It was early morning in Vancouver and, given the sounds in the background, Jack must be at the office. He could dodge my calls; I didn't have the mental fortitude to keep my temper if he did. So, I sent a text saying that I'd be out of contact for a few hours. He couldn't argue if he didn't acknowledge me.

I might not know how to start, but the lack of ransom demand took away a little urgency. If I didn't sleep now, I'd be making bad decisions from exhaustion. The pharmacy sold sleeping pills as well as No Doz, so I'd stocked up for whatever came at me.

While I couldn't do anything active now, I could make a head start. So far, the time difference had been a barrier, but it could be a tool. In Vancouver someone had a whole day to find me help. One of the benefits of my line of work was the variety of people you meet. Not everyone with secrets was a criminal, not everyone who dabbled in the dark side was a bad person. Those were my contacts. People who could find out who knew what and would share it with someone they trusted.

Most of my connections were kept more than arm's length from the law firm. But, one of them sat smack in the middle of it. And unlike the others, he had an international past along with a lot of secrets.

Michael Okonkwo worked for Hennessy, Rogers & Lawson. They hired him as a tech specialist. And officially, he analyzed the flow of information around a case and pointed out where the client might be vulnerable. More specifically he dug around until he could be sure where the firm might be taking more of a risk than they expected. He tracked phone records regardless of the legality of the search and never got caught, and he'd hacked a few emails for me. He was a friend as well as a resource. I'd miss him when I disappeared.

In my current circumstance, I needed his network to navigate the local criminal scene. If he came to help me, it would be the best thing. It would take too long to travel here and if the ransom request came through while he flew here, I'd be in worse shape than now.

Michael didn't talk much about why he left Nigeria, but one night over a bottle of tequila he told me a few stories. He'd traveled by stowing away, hitch-hiking, and walking across Europe before landing a flight to Canada and a work visa. With no money, a lot of charm, and low barriers to making friends and allies, he built a network of petty criminals and radicals along the way. I knew because he'd used them a few times to secure information, pictures, or files to close a case. Right now, I didn't care if he sent me a criminal to help, and maybe that would be best.

I left a message for Michael to call me in a couple of hours, saying it was urgent and I needed a contact in

Prague, but no other details. Then I took the sleeping pill, lay on the bed, and fell asleep.

THE PILLS WORKED AMAZINGLY WELL. No dreams, or at least none I remember, and when my phone woke me, I was alert and mostly clear headed.

"Michael?" The word came out a bit thick. I needed to brush my teeth and take in some caffeine to cut through the remaining fuzz in my mind. I wanted it delivered in the form of coffee, not pills, at least not yet. "I need someone I can trust over here," I said. "Oh yeah, and hi."

"The vacation must be getting interesting if you need a contact. Can you tell me more?"

I hated not bringing him in on the case, but if things went sideways, I wanted him to be insulated from the fall-out. If I told him about the kidnapping, I'd have to tell him why Jack had leverage and I wouldn't be there to stop him fixing things for me.

"I picked up a job." The truth at least.

"How, if you don't have any contacts?" His deep voice was heavy with accusation. He knew I was holding back. If he thought I couldn't handle it, he'd refuse to help until he had the whole story. I loved him like a brother, but he had a different idea about protecting family than I had.

Our usual bickering about letting me take care of myself was a waste of time when we couldn't do it over a drink. And he was just trying to find the right contact and not be nosy, I truly believed that. But I couldn't answer, and I didn't have the energy or clarity of mind to dodge questions without increasing his suspicions. I had to be clear up front about the lines around this particular case.

"You don't want me to tell you," I said. "I need someone who can find their way around the criminal element. The people I'm looking for are definitely on the wrong side of the law."

"I've been texting people to see who's available." He answered someone who interrupted him with a business question. "I already figured you weren't looking for a tour guide. If you can't tell me any details, I can't guarantee it's the right contact, and..."

"And what?" I hoped I could work with whoever he sent me. I needed a link to the right places, and maybe a translator, and that was all.

"Nothing," he said. "I need more, Sharka. If I make the wrong connection, I risk losing you and a good contact."

I checked the time; 6 PM. It would still be morning in Vancouver, but the nap had staved off the worst of the jet lag. "I can't. You need deniability."

He muttered something to the person in the room then came back to the phone. "Okay, I'm alone. You don't need to worry about protecting me. I've survived so far, and you know my network didn't come from Craigslist. Let me help you."

"I need to think about it." The fact that he had multiple contacts shouldn't have surprised me. And he wouldn't be clean of whatever they did. But I needed to brush my teeth and shower some sense into my brain before I decided to bring him in on the details. "I think you have enough to help. I need a connection to the darker side of Prague. You know what I can do, so you understand who I need."

"Fine, I guess I appreciate the thought. The guy I'm thinking of doesn't like to have his decisions questioned, or any nosing around his past. Can you manage that without punching him?"

"As long as he helps, I'll restrain my better instincts for you. Call me when he agrees. Let me know what he costs."

"Okay. Be careful." He disconnected.

Not being out there looking for Rio was starting to rankle, which was another bad sign. If I rushed, we'd both probably end up dead; or she'd be dead, and I'd have to live with the mistake.

Fifteen minutes later I was showered and ready to go, but I still didn't have my contact, or any information to tell me where to go.

One thing I could do while I waited was orient myself to the city; some might call it sightseeing. I'd never had to do any kind of job in a place I couldn't navigate, and I suspected that would be a huge mistake.

Michael called back as I downloaded some maps to find a restaurant.

"You'll get a call or text from a guy named Radim."

"Thanks." I didn't want to wait for him to make contact. "Give me his details and I'll reach out."

"Not how this works," Michael said. "He is in control until you meet."

"I don't have a lot of time, here." It was a stupid thing to say. I wouldn't have asked for help if I had time to find my own.

"You need to give me a reason to break my rules."

"You won't want to know," I said. Maybe I had it wrong. Feeling isolated should make me reach out for help, so why did it feel like I had to push everyone away?

"Don't you trust me?"

It wasn't about trust. Normally I would stand firm. But there were too many priorities pulling at me. Jack's problem forced me to look for assistance. My plans needed me to be alone to work. "I'm trying to protect you."

"I don't need that, and I'm insulted that you think I do," Michael said.

He joked, but the words made me sit and take a breath. "Believe me, you do. You think you can take care of yourself, but this is bigger than most cases we handle."

"Okay, then you wait for him to contact you. It won't be long, Sharka."

The statement was supposed to end the argument, but it just made me realize I was being stupid. I needed someone to watch Jack. I couldn't trust him not to screw everything up at the last minute. Even a text or call at the wrong time might cost Rio her life.

For Michael to do that for me, he deserved a reason why.

"Here it is. I'm doing Jack a favor," I said. "His daughter, she's been taken, and he wants me to find her."

"You hinted that I'd regret asking for details." Michael laughed. "So, no cops?"

"I tried to get him to call them, but he won't. I think he's hiding something."

Every sensible part of me wanted to tell Michael what was going on — the little I had. Without the knowledge, how would he be sure that this Radim was the right help? But that small voice in the back of my brain I called my gut shouted at me to protect him; that this was more than what Jack told me. Even knowing I was not in the best shape to make decisions, I knew not to completely ignore the voice.

"You want me to find out why?" He sounded eager to get involved. That had to stop.

"No. It's too dangerous. I just want to know if Jack is acting odd or goes missing." Although he's always secretive and controlling, maybe the stress of Rio's situation would make him less cautious.

"Yeah, well, he's acting wrong right now. For a guy whose daughter is in danger, he's being pretty much like himself."

I thought back to our call. He'd been angry, more than angry, but I couldn't figure out why. Maybe it was just how he showed fear?

"Like that," I said. "Don't tell anyone what's going on. It's going to be hard enough to find her without having the cops show up without warning."

"I'll add it to the list of secrets I'm holding," Michael said. "I'll see if I can pull some information to help you."

"Just be careful," I said. Michael was the closest I had to a friend and I was about to abandon him. I felt like a shit but hoped eventually he'd realize why and forgive me.

"Trust Radim. He'll know who to talk to," Michael said. "Got to go, be safe."

"Wait, what about the contact information?"

"Not a chance. I promise you'll understand someday," he said.

"I'm not a kid asking about sex." But that's exactly what I heard in his voice. *You'll understand when you grow up.*

"I hope you never get to the point where you value the way I protect my network. No more arguments. And you'll owe me a fancy meal when you get back."

Then he was gone.

I'd have to find another way to pay him back. I wasn't planning on returning to Vancouver no matter what happened with Rio.

Chapter 5

A couple of hours later I had a good idea how to get around the city on foot. I'd eaten a pizza that put ours to shame and tasted a chocolate that made me fall in love. It had been hard to resist a beer, but I needed to be alert, and beer tended to make me tipsier than wine. And I had more sense than to add alcohol or a hit of caffeine to the residual of the sleeping pill.

In my walk, I'd seen the famous clock and famous bridge and strolled along the waterfront. Everything I saw made me wish Jack hadn't called. As a tourist I'd have explored more of the history, so I would recognize the statues on the bridge, and lingered to soak up the views. Maybe when I finished the job, I would do that. Kind of dipping my toe into this quiet life I wanted.

Now it was too late to head to the famous castle, so the waterfront was my best option. From there I could reach most of the city by bus or taxi or, if I had time, by walking.

A group of rowdy men with Australian accents celebrating a stag night passed by. A cover artist from a night-club across the street sang a soundtrack to my walk. The crowds were milling around food stands without pushing anyone or starting fights. There was something about the city that felt comfortable and safe. It probably was safe for the tourists around me as long as they guarded against pickpockets. Rio must have thought the same thing and now she'd learned that despite the atmosphere of community, crime happened everywhere.

My phone rang, dragging me back from my imagination to the real Prague. The caller ID was blocked. "Hello?"

"You are Michael's friend?" a man asked.

"Yes, and you?"

"Also a friend. Come to me. Walk. It will be faster."

How could he be certain where I was? "I could take a cab," I said, not wanting to delay.

"A taxi will take advantage of you unless a hotel or restaurant calls, which leaves a record to be followed up on. Walk."

I stifled my urge to argue and remembered Michael chose this guy. "Okay. Where?"

"*U Konci.* It is what you would call a pub, yes?"

"Sure." I had no idea. Granny didn't frequent pubs, so I didn't recognize the word. "What's the address?" I had no clue how to spell the name for my app to find the location, and asking questions made me feel like I was more in control of the situation.

He gave me the street name and a few landmarks. "You will find me easy."

The street was in New Town, according to my map. "I'm on the waterfront, not far from the Charles Bridge." Maybe he would give me a hint on direction.

"Yes, easy to find. See you in fifteen minutes. You like beer?"

It had been long enough that my system should be

clear of the sleeping pill and I didn't have to drink it. Having him buy me a beer might be a good step in forming a working relationship. "Yes, dark beer."

"A pint of *Černé Pivo* will be waiting."

I leaned against the stone railing and looked closely at the map on my phone. I tried to type in the road to get a start, but the app needed more information to give me directions. I zoomed in and found the street. Fifteen minutes would be easy. I could stay along the waterfront for most of the walk. I guessed at where to turn away from the river. From that point, I'd see if he was right about finding the landmarks. I muttered the name he gave me a few times, hoping I would recognize the sign.

I guess there wouldn't be too many guys with an extra dark beer waiting, so identifying Radim might be the easiest part.

I FOUND THE PUB EASILY. Three young men each with a beer in hand stood outside, talking quietly under a notice that said the patio closed about half an hour ago. They said hi as I walked past, and I gave them a smile.

There were only two tables for customers inside the door, both empty. A waitress looked up from behind the bar. "Yes. Go downstairs please."

She pointed to the back of the pub. It was dark. I looked back at her. She nodded and pointed again.

I tried to look confident as I headed into the shadows. It wasn't the first time I'd had to act like I knew what I was doing. It was a skill I relied on to save my life a time or two.

A few steps in, I reached the top of a staircase twisting down into a bright basement. A group of people sat in front of a widescreen TV, yelling at a soccer game. A couple at a table in the back were intent on each other and didn't even know anyone was in the room with them.

I walked around a corner and found a few more tables. One held a man who had a half-drunk beer in his hand and a full pint of dark beer on the table in front of him. He looked at me over his glass and glanced away.

In his fifties and lean as a marathon runner, he had blue eyes that took in everything at once. His wide cheekbones and slow smile must have made him quite a player in his youth — maybe now too. He wore jeans, a faded green tee-shirt and boots. He kept his eyes on the wall mural of a pastoral scene, but he knew I was here. The smile told me that. I liked that he was willing to wait for me to make the first move.

I did just that. "Radim?"

He nodded.

I sat in the chair and tasted the beer. It was as good as I expected from the color. "What did Michael tell you?"

"Not so quick," he said.

The waitress joined us, and he ordered two more beers.

"I'm not sure that's a good idea," I said.

"Drink or don't drink," he said. "This is a business and we don't want to stand out by not ordering."

I couldn't argue. I took another sip.

"Your name: Sharka. You are Czech?"

"My family," I said. "Does it matter?"

"No. Michael said you need help. What with?"

The waitress deposited our beers and Radim paid.

"I don't want Michael knowing any more details than I gave him. It could put him in a tricky place, or in trouble he can't wiggle out of."

"And me? Getting strangers in trouble is okay?"

This guy was rubbing me the wrong way already. I wasn't here to make a friend. He was supposed to be helping me, not annoying me. I restrained my urge to leave him right then. I might be running out of time to pick a partner with better people skills.

"I got the feeling it wouldn't be the first time," I said. "You seem like the kind of person who handles trouble well."

That brought out his smile and smoothed out my raw nerves.

"Okay, what's the job?"

"A girl has been kidnapped. Her father is reluctant to get the police involved." I left out the fact that Jack's way of dealing with it bothered me.

"Who is she? Why is she here?"

"Will you help?"

He downed the last of his beer. "You tell me what you know and then go back to your vacation. I'll take care of it."

I wasn't going to be shoved aside like I didn't know how to find Rio, which I admit I didn't. I had to do this for Jack. I couldn't give him any avenue to wiggle out of our agreement. "No. You are here to help me."

"My contacts won't talk to you." He folded his arms across his chest and kept his eyes on me.

I sensed a test. Was he trying to find my weakness, so he could take over? Would that be a better thing for Rio? Maybe, but she wasn't the only one with something to lose.

"I'll be present when they talk to you. I'm not stepping back from this." I couldn't afford to step back. I wasn't going to hand Jack any reason to go back on his promise. When I had Rio, I'd have leverage. He spills my secret, I tell everyone he put his daughter's life in danger to save a few million.

"What makes you think you can find her?" he finally asked.

"I'm an investigator. I know what to do, I just need an in with the locals."

He leaned forward. "Police? Michael should have said."

"No. Private. I work with Michael sometimes."

I let him think it over and drank my beer. The soccer game must have ended because I heard chairs scraping and people leaving. They were pretty quiet, so I figured their team lost.

"If I tell you it's too dangerous, you don't argue." He waited for me to agree.

I nodded. He didn't need to know I'd break that promise if he tried to keep me too far from the action.

"You don't ask for names when you meet my people. If they want to stay anonymous, you respect that."

"I don't need names or anything about who they are, or why they are helping." I put the empty glass down. "Look. I'm good with following your lead when I can tell you're more experienced than me, but don't forget I'm in charge. What's your rate?"

"I owe Michael. When we are done you owe me. Just pay the bills from now until we are finished."

It was a very loose agreement, but I could live with a grey area. If I owed him a favor in the future, he'd need to find me to collect. "Okay."

"Tell me everything you know."

I gave him the few details Jack had passed on, keeping back the blackmail. Radim didn't need to know I was forced to do this.

"Okay." He sent a text and then dropped the phone into his pocket. "Come, the night is early. Let me show you the city."

There was no reason to stay here and keep drinking, so I followed him back to the street.

. . .

PRAGUE DIDN'T SLOW down at night. Radim led me to the lower level of the waterfront. He called it the River Walk. The walkway was lined with barges more like nightclubs than restaurants, despite their names. The chatter and bustle of the people restored some of my vitality. One thing I did notice was that the beer hadn't affected me as much as I thought. Instead of feeling fuzzy, I found a well of energy.

"Why don't we find somewhere to sit down?" I said. "And how do we know we're walking in the right direction, or that the call is going to come in soon enough?"

Radim didn't answer me. He just sped up. It wasn't like he ran, but I definitely felt he was trying to take the lead. Good thing my legs were long enough to keep up without looking like a fool.

"Where are we heading?"

He came to a stop, and I walked a few steps past him before I realized.

"I don't like to stay in one place for too long," he said. "Why do you need to know where we're going? If I told you, how would you use this information?"

He had a point. I'd only been here for about six hours. And I was under no illusion my short scoping out of the city was going to make me able to chase someone around without losing them within the first minute. "If you're just going to walk and make me follow, then I'm not going to get to know the place at all."

"You won't know the city well enough to do this job without me."

I had no plans to ditch him; I knew the value of local contacts. But this was my case, my freedom, my secret. "Maybe we'll be separated, maybe that won't happen," I said. "But why don't you tell me anyway? We don't want the girl to die because I'm stuck in a part of the city I can't navigate."

He looked up and down the River Walk, as though expecting to catch someone tailing us. I followed his actions and saw nothing but crowds of partiers.

"We don't know what information is coming," he said, taking my arm. We started walking again. "We're going to walk while we wait. I won't take us too far away from the center. But it is possible they took her away from Prague. Then it doesn't matter where we are when the call comes."

I didn't want to think about that. Europe was a big place to search if they moved Rio. "So where are we going?"

"We go to Lesser Town. Across the Charles. Lots of tourists means we can hide in a crowd."

It also meant bad things could happen to us, without anyone noticing. It's not like we were walking along with the church group here. Almost everyone had the slightly glassy look that came after a night of one too many drinks. But if he thought we were going to be safer here, at least for now, I would trust him.

We wove through the clusters of people, retracing my steps from earlier in the evening to reach the entrance of the Charles Bridge.

A sea of people walked toward us. Although I knew it looked denser than it actually was, I still braced for a struggle to get through. Radim led me down the center of the bridge, pointing out features I barely listened to. Some saint, some guy who'd been killed on the bridge. Some other saint. Like most statues, they all came with a story. If he told me every piece of history or legend, it would take us an hour to cross. "I'm not here as a tourist."

He laughed, suddenly making me feel more like part of the crowd than someone using it for cover.

"Unless you've lived here through everything my people have experienced, you're a tourist. Maybe you'll learn your way around the city better, but our history ties us together. We've all done something in the past that needs to stay in the past."

He had no idea how well I understood his words.

Chapter 6

We sat in a quiet park across the river. The only other people here were busy with their own business, mostly young people expressing their feelings for each other in non-verbal ways.

I was still pissed at him for treating me like I didn't have a clue what I was doing just because I hadn't been here when they were occupied. No matter how many times I tried to be professional, I couldn't quite rid myself of the feeling he was humoring me.

"What did you investigate for this law firm?" he asked, surprising me by breaking the silence.

"Whatever they needed."

He shrugged. "You don't want to talk?"

I looked around me. The Lennon Wall stood just off to my right. I could see the graffiti. The riotous color and uncensored messages would definitely upset the communists. The top layers of paint were not that old. I guess nothing is so good someone doesn't think they can make it better. "Can you reach out to your contact again?"

"There is still time," he said. "These kidnappers are not in a hurry. Why do you think that is?"

The question worried me too. Kidnapping was a fast turnaround crime. The longer they kept the hostage, the easier it would be for her to identify them later. "I don't want to work on their timeline."

"Sometimes patience is the best way," he said. "You don't like me. Why?"

"I don't know you and you don't know me. We have a hard job to do and the risk is higher if we can't trust each other."

"You don't trust Michael knows what he's doing?"

I rubbed my face. The peacefulness was lulling me back to sleep. "Yes, but how long has it been since he worked with you?" I didn't care about what they'd done, but if Michael hadn't connected with Radim in years, maybe he didn't know the man as well as he thought.

"We speak," Radim said. "How long since you worked with him?"

"Last week," I said.

"You win." He leaned back and supported himself on his elbows. "Try to enjoy this peace. When we learn more about this girl's situation, there will be no time to rest."

I knew that. What bothered me was the suspicion that if I fell asleep, he'd leave me here and go after the kidnappers by himself. Maybe Radim doing the rescue would work out for Rio, but not for me.

"Why do you think I don't know what I'm supposed to do?" I asked more to keep the conversation going than to get a true answer. I had to be more familiar with him to tell when he lied and that took time. Until then, I'd assume he was withholding something if not outright lying. Trust was not one of my strengths and I didn't expect that to change any time soon.

"I don't know you," he said with a laugh. "We are alike, perhaps enough to help us in this case."

His laugh released some of the tension. Losing the heavy suspicion made me realize if I couldn't find a way to trust him, I'd ditch him. I'd have to ask for another contact from Michael and start again with someone new and maybe worse than Radim.

"Tell me one thing about you that will make me feel differently," I said.

"And will you do the same?" He sat up and looked directly at me.

His intent gaze made me uncomfortable and I almost said no. But trust worked both ways, so I took a breath and said, "Yes. You go first."

He smiled. "I like jazz."

I laughed. "Rock and roll. Perhaps we are destined to be enemies."

"Perhaps not. Music is not the only place to look for commonality." He stared up at the sky. "We start again, yes?"

"Okay. Hi, my name is Sharka Lewis. I need your help." Dropping everything up to now was impossible, but if I pretended I trusted him, maybe I would eventually.

"Radim Stipek," he said. "Whatever skills I possess are yours."

I figured he was holding back as much as I was, but when he wasn't trying to take over, he was a pretty good guy.

Radim's phone pinged as we were shaking hands on our new start. He pulled it out and showed me a text.

"I don't read Czech," I said. I never thought I'd miss the overly emoji'd texts from friends.

"I do," he said, but didn't translate the words. Another text came in with a video link before I could prompt him.

He held the phone so I could see, then tapped the icon.

The shot was grainy black and white, a security camera recording; a dark street somewhere in a city. I prayed it was in Prague. A door opened, pouring light into the street for a moment, then Rio stepped through and closed it.

Knowing what happened, I couldn't stop my brain looking for all the signs she should have noticed, something that would alert her and send her inside to safety.

A car drove past as Rio stopped to light a cigarette. A van pulled up across the street.

Two men got out. Rio took a drag and started to walk, oblivious to what was coming.

One of the men circled around behind her, the other ran toward her.

I held my breath as we watched them grab her. She tried to fight her way free, stubbing her cigarette into the first man's arm, but he didn't let go.

She tried to scream, and the second man held a rag across her mouth.

Rio bucked and kicked, but too late. The drug slowed her down, reducing the force behind her fists. In moments she collapsed.

The men lifted her and took her to the back of the van.

We couldn't see what they did, but they weren't out of camera for long enough to do more than toss her in the back.

The passenger jumped in and the van started up. The video ended.

"No license plate," I said.

"That would take the challenge away," Radim said. He showed me the next text.

"I still can't read Czech."

"He found no other sightings," Radim said. "He will continue to look."

"How did your friend find this? We gave him no information."

"He found her on the register of the university. Then he scanned everything he could find in the area."

"Do you know where she is?" I assumed the contact was hacking into whatever video records he could find. If Jack would listen to reason and bring in the cops, what we had should make them move fast.

"I know the street. It's a private university, I think. Her father has money?"

"And he's not ready to pay the ransom yet," I said, hoping Jack wasn't going to refuse to pay ever.

"Perhaps that is wise," he said. "My friend will tell us if he gets more to help."

"So that's all?" I stood, my body wanted to go after the van as if the event had happened in the park.

"For now," Radim said. "I have other friends. Was she a student?"

"Yes," I said. "Do your other friends hack into cameras?"

He typed. "Not just cameras." He sent the text.

"We should go to the university," I said.

"Yes," Radim said. "There may be something we can find to tell us why they took her."

His phone pinged. He glanced at the screen. "We need her passwords."

"I can ask her father." I didn't hold out too much hope.

"Does your father hold your passwords?"

"He's dead." I hadn't meant to be so short with him. "I don't know who else might have hers."

"Okay, there is time." He typed another text. "This is

not something we need to ask him. I have many friends, remember?"

"I do. Can we go now?"

"It is not always necessary for us to act, Sharka. You know that."

I felt like I'd waited for long enough. "I don't think we'll find her by sitting in a park."

"Yes, that would be too easy." He started walking to the steps that would take us to the bridge. "Come on. We'll go to the university to see if there are some clues for us."

Chapter 7

I followed Radim back toward the Old Town Square. The crowds thinned as we left the bridge area, but people still walked home from clubs, or whatever stayed open late here.

"Why wouldn't people be around when they took her?" I asked. "Are the streets ever deserted like that?"

"You think they made that happen?" Radim asked as he turned down a side street before we reached the square. "Blocked the cars?"

"Would they have to?" The streets were getting narrower and if a car came along, we'd be forced to press against a wall to make room. I only hoped the road was one way.

"I don't think so," he said. "See how quiet it is now?"

Radim came to a stop at a door set in a building that looked a thousand years old. I checked up and down the street. The university took up most of the left side of the road, and shuttered shops lined the right side. The ones I could identify ranged from small grocery stores to tourist traps selling marionettes. We were the only people here.

"We're about an hour earlier than the kidnapping," I said.

I moved to where Rio had stopped to light the cigarette. The road got slightly wider here because of a driveway into the grounds. That wasn't something we could tell from the video. I located the camera high on the wall opposite. I didn't recognize the store.

"Why would they need a camera?" Probably nothing that would help, but more information wouldn't hurt. We didn't have anything else to work with, so I couldn't let this one clue go without draining everything from it.

"A bank," Radim said. "The kind that keeps its clients secret. They want to know who is outside before they allow entry."

Could that have something to do with Rio? "Criminals?"

"It is possible," Radim said. "Not many know about it. The government pretends to ignore what they do for their clients."

I'd run across that kind of bank before. Getting access to any more of the footage from a few days before to see if they cased the place would be impossible unless Radim's contact could hack again. I could do some research on my own as well to find out if it was relevant. "Could your friend get more video?"

"He said they shut him out. I think that means no."

I hoped the next clues we found weren't cut off so short. "We should try to get inside the university."

"No one will be there." He crossed to inspect the door anyway.

If I'd known I was going to be working on my vacation, I'd have packed my picks. Or perhaps not. TSA wouldn't appreciate finding them in my checked luggage and no way would they allow them in carry-on. "Shouldn't there be a buzzer?"

"I don't see one," he said.

I watched him run his finger around the edge of the door. Heavy wood with metal fixtures. Not unusual, as most of the doors here looked sturdy enough to repel invaders, but why would a university need to be impenetrable and yet not install a camera? As far as I could tell, they couldn't know from their own security measures that Rio was taken.

"Keypad," Radim said, breaking into my thoughts. "Student access."

I stepped around him and banged my fist on the wood. "Maybe they like the old ways," I said, pressing my ear against the door.

"You won't hear," Radim said.

I shrugged. "I need to do something, and it doesn't hurt to try."

When it was obvious that no one was coming, I crossed the street for a better view of the building. The only windows were too high up to make climbing easy. "Is this the only door?"

Radim joined me. "A front door," he said. "What kind of university is it?"

"You mean what kind of university needs to be inside a fortress?"

"This is Prague," he said. "We use what is available."

"I don't think Jack would have sent his daughter to someplace shady," I said. I pushed off from the wall. "Let's try the other door."

"After we do, you rest," he said. "Tomorrow we make more progress."

"We could hardly make less." As much as I wanted to keep kicking doors until we found Rio, I knew it was useless. A couple of hours' research without Radim pointing out my shortcomings might help.

We walked around the building to find the front entrance. Not much more welcoming than the side one. More windows, but still high up. Lighting around the door helped us read the notice that said the university was closed from midnight to nine AM. No buzzer, no keypad, a cover locked over the keyhole.

"Tomorrow it is," I said.

"I will walk with you to your hotel," Radim said.

"No need." I knew the way, and it was along nicely lit streets, and I wanted to keep a little distance from him until I got more comfortable with him, until he earned a little trust. "Will you be at the entrance when they open?" I would be.

"Tomorrow," Radim said. Not really answering my question. "Sleep. You will be no use if you don't."

"What will you do?"

"I might talk to a few friends, but I need rest too."

"If you learn anything, you call," I said.

"I promise I won't find the girl without you." He smiled. It didn't take the sting out. "You must rest, Sharka."

I must have looked like hell if he insisted I stop. My body wouldn't let me argue with him. I had that hollow feeling that came with exhaustion. "Fine. I'll rest up." I waved goodbye and headed confidently towards the Old Town Square. I could easily find my bearings from there.

Back in my room, I sat on the bed in my pajamas, under no illusion that I had any chance of staying awake. I set my alarm for six AM to give me time for more work before breakfast.

Since I had limited time to research, I started with Rio's social media. The big three, Facebook, Instagram, and Twitter gave me an insight into her life here. She had little to say on Facebook, mostly reposts from quizzes and other friends. She rarely tweeted anything about herself, of course if she was an active tweeter, I would be drowning in posts. I followed her on Instagram and crossed my fingers. Lots of pictures; a typical member of her generation and if I was younger, I might have thought to start there.

I scanned the recent photos, hoping to see repeated faces in the background, but if she was being stalked, then it was by a pro. I went back a month on just the images and then worked forward, reading the captions.

She poked fun at herself for revisiting the tourist sites, suggesting she would fall back on guiding if her major failed. She took a few pictures of her work area with captions about how it was her new home, all ending in 'lol'. Not all the shots were selfies. It was good to see her before the terror and beating. She dressed in jeans and shirts, sometimes layered skirts and off the shoulder tee-shirts — kind of a blend between hippie and Madonna chic. She still had the tattoo of a dove just above her collarbone. She'd pierced her nose and lip, I'm guessing in rebellion against her father's conservative lifestyle.

My vision blurred, and sleep was only a blink away. Oddly, it helped like one of those 3D pictures, and details popped out. I noticed in five of the most recent posts, the same man lurking in the background. To be honest, the lurking was more like standing, and he wasn't always looking at her, but five times couldn't be a coincidence.

I used my phone to take a picture of the screen because I needed faster access than flipping through her posts to show Radim what I found. Then I rubbed my eyes and turned to some Google searches.

Rio majored in data analysis. Not your garden variety of finding connections for targeting ads. I had to look up some terms to get a clue, and even then, I didn't truly understand what it meant.

She studied the flow of information and something called data farming. Why couldn't she dumb it down on social media? Most people did. But maybe she had, and this was another piece of proof that I was more clueless than the average teenager.

After following links and making notes until my eyes kept closing on me, I'd gleaned that she was trying to create a process, or an app, to gather data for use by law enforcement.

Then I jerked awake with my hands on the keyboard and drool on my chin. I folded the laptop closed and curled up to sleep, hoping tomorrow Rio would be doing the same.

Chapter 8

The next morning came too fast. I desperately wanted to hit the snooze button, but if I did, I wouldn't have time to follow up on some of the details from last night. Like the mystery man I found. I tried to call Jack to ask if he had someone watching Rio, someone who'd failed at the job, but he didn't answer. I left a message and got ready for the day. After I dressed, I sent Michael a text asking if he knew anything about what Rio was studying and headed down for breakfast.

The buffet was almost all meat. I stuck a slice of bread in the toaster, loaded my plate with sausage and pickles and turned to find a table. Radim sat at the one closest to the back wall. No one sat nearby. Of course, it might be the way he filled the space with brooding menace.

I poured a coffee and joined him. "How did you know where I was staying?" I was impressed as well as annoyed he'd found me so easily. He didn't need to find out about the impressed part.

"I have friends," he said. "You should try the cheese." He picked up a wedge from his plate.

"I'll start with this," I said. I heard the toaster pop and left him to retrieve the rest of my breakfast.

When I got back, he raised his coffee cup like a glass of wine. "Today we will find what this Rio was working on. Perhaps it will shine a light on the reason for her kidnapping."

How could he be so optimistic? This case could grind on for days.

"How much do you know about how data flows?" I asked.

"Not much," he said. "Is that what she did? Searched through streams of little pieces of information to find answers?"

It surprised me that he hadn't found it out the same way I had. "Yes. Do you or any of your friends know how to interpret that stuff?"

He pulled his phone from his pocket. "I will see. But I do have her passwords. We can hope to find enlightenment in her accounts."

Maybe he did know the right kind of people for this. "What passwords?"

He unlocked his phone and showed me the screen. "The ones for her studies. Her bank took a little longer because she hid it better. Is there something else we need?"

I couldn't answer until we'd looked at her accounts and into what she was studying. "Have you looked at any of it?"

He finished his last bite and gestured for me to eat up. "We must go to the university to use her passwords there. Her online bank statements didn't show anything unusual. We need time to dig past the list of transactions."

The university wouldn't be open for another ninety minutes. "Tell me what you saw."

He left to refill his coffee. The server cleared his plate away. I still had half my food to go. My normal breakfast was just toast and coffee. I might need to rethink that; salamis and pickles might be a better start to my day.

"Okay," Radim said, settling across from me. "Every month, Daddy puts money in the account and Rio takes part of the balance. I have a friend trying to track where the rest goes. No transfers for rent or phone. She lives on cash, not usual for young people to do."

"How can you be certain the funds come from Jack?"

"He did not hide it."

"You hacked into his account?" How would Jack take that?

"Only to the one he uses to pay her. Money goes in there and then out to her. One more transaction started two weeks ago. We are trying to get access to the records."

"So, not to Rio?"

"Until we can get into the account, I don't speculate."

"He's smart." At a minimum Jack would own hundreds of accounts, each one for a specific purpose, so it meant the transaction was likely going to an account for Rio.

"Not so smart. We need more time to find where he gets the money to fund her," Radim said. "Should we keep going?"

Did I believe looking at Jack's banking transactions would help us find Rio? More than likely it would be a distraction. "Not now."

"Time to go," Radim said, standing.

"The university doesn't open for another hour," I said. "We can talk here."

"No," he said. "Time to move on."

I drank the last of my coffee. "Do we have time for me to pick something up from my room?"

"I'll wait outside," Radim said. Then he left.

The server hovered at my table. "You sign for the breakfast, please."

She presented a receipt. Guest meals weren't included in my reservation. I filled in my room number and signed the chit. If Radim cost me only a few meals, I wasn't going to argue.

Passing through the lobby to the elevator, I saw him standing next to the door, talking on his phone. Was he making arrangements for more help from his multitude of friends?

I didn't need to pick anything up from my room; I wasn't going to wander around the city with Radim until the university opened. I hit the toilet and then organized my things for the day. One credit card, some cash, my phone and room card. All in pockets, no need for a purse to get in my way.

When I got back to the lobby, Radim had disappeared. I hurried to the door and stepped out. He stood across the street, talking to a young woman dressed in period costume. My phone rang as I crossed to join them.

I checked the caller ID: Jack. Could I ignore him? Yes, but I shouldn't, and I'd miss a good opportunity to ask about the transactions.

"Yes?" I was not in the mood for a cheerful greeting. Radim noticed me. I held up a hand to let him know I needed a minute.

"You haven't called with a progress report."

I guess I wasn't the only one feeling irritated.

"There's nothing to report." Not quite true but I didn't want to open with questions, and other than that, I had nothing.

"What have you been doing, then?"

"Jack, it takes time. Did they contact you? Do you have anything to help us?"

He didn't answer, and I was tempted to pretend we'd

been cut off, but he would just call back, so I kept talking. "Jack? We're going to review what she was studying."

"Why haven't you done that already? I'm not paying you to sit around."

So, he was paying me to talk to him? "What time is it there?"

"What does it matter?"

"It's morning here. That means we couldn't have done anything until now. The university was closed."

Radim joined me.

"I could have arranged for you to get in," Jack said. "I pay enough fucking money in fees. If you had bothered to call me, I would have forced someone to open the doors."

Good to know, but not believable since he ignored my message earlier. "I'll keep that in mind," I said. "But we're heading there now."

"I expect you to tell me what you find. Remember the stakes here. I can make your secret public at any time."

The threat was just bluster. If he outed me, I had no reason to keep looking for Rio. Not that I could walk away, but I had enough money to fund my future. Jack would never trace the location of what he paid. He outs me, and I tell the police what really happened. But I'd had enough sleep to be sure it wasn't a conversation to get into right now. He'd been awake all this time, presumably worrying about his daughter.

"We're nine hours out of sync, Jack," I said in what I thought was a reasonable tone.

"Don't make excuses," he snarled. "Find Rio and the people who took her."

I held the phone out and glared at it. I could hear him swearing at me and waited until he ran out of steam. "Get some rest," I said. "Take a pill if you need to. I can't do the job with you looking over my shoulder. I can't do the job without something to show me where to go next. If you keep yelling at me, you'll hold up the investigation. I'll call you when I have something to tell you, or when I need something from you." My questions could wait until we had something good to report.

"I'll call you whenever I want," he said.

"And if you do when I'm sneaking up on the kidnappers, you'll blow it. They'll kill your daughter and that can't be fixed with money." I ended the call before I had to listen to more of his ranting. Then I put the phone on silent mode.

"The father?" Radim asked.

"He's worried." I didn't believe fear for Rio explained it all, but Radim didn't need to listen to my complaining about an asshole I was never going to see again.

"Will he interfere?"

"I'll handle him." I checked the time before I dropped my phone into my pocket. "We should go. The doors will open in a half hour."

It was a short walk, but my phone had vibrated seven times as Jack tried to reach me. The university doors were open by the time we arrived. Thankfully this was an urban campus, no grounds except for the gated approach, no maze of buildings to search through.

A young man with the slightly bewildered look of an academic waited outside. He wore jeans, a striped shirt and a black hoodie, and stepped toward us as we approached.

"Petr Zajic," he said, holding his hand out to shake mine.

"A friend," Radim said as I told Petr my name.

"Come in," Petr said. "It is quieter inside. I can show you where Rio worked."

My brain took a moment to adjust when we stepped through. Open spaces, bright chairs and tables, and wide stairs replaced the ancient look of the building. The modern encased in the classic.

"Did you know her?" I asked. "Rio?"

"A little. It's a small university and we were studying the same discipline."

He was forthcoming enough to make me optimistic he'd be able to tell us more about her work. "Did you share research?"

"Come, sit," Petr said. "We will be more comfortable."

Another little delay, but I knew the value of letting a source control the pace of an interview. Although, nothing about this felt like an interview. It was more like a visit.

"You know that she is missing, yes?" Radim asked.

Petr shrugged. "We come and go as we need to. She is off at some music festival in Germany, or somewhere else."

"Did she do that often?" It was tricky trying to figure out if his lack of concern came from belief in what he said, or if he was part of the crew who took her. I hated having to rely on Radim's mysterious contacts.

"We all wander a little," Petr said. "Our work can be dull at times. We need a break."

"What was she working on?" I asked. "I don't really understand her specialty."

"She is brilliant," Petr said. This time his face lit up with admiration. "I have trouble following her thoughts and I'm three years longer in the study. She's preparing the ground for a PhD. Not for a few years, she says, but she planned to fast-track. Is that the right expression?"

"Isn't she too young for that?" PhD was the last degree you got, as far as I knew. She was still a teenager, and brilliance didn't always correlate with maturity.

"Yes, too young, but as I said, brilliant. And when you are touched by that, you must act when you are young for fear the magic will fade."

Okay, so we were dealing with a genius. That didn't bode well for me understanding the work enough to learn why she was taken. "But you can explain her research," I said.

"Yes. Not completely, but enough, I think." Petr leaned forward. "She was looking for a way to follow money as it moved."

"The cops can do that now," I said.

Radim narrowed his eyes like he wanted me to stop interrupting.

"Yes, you are right, but Rio wanted to track in real time. To watch the money as it moved, not to look back after. Once money is traveling, it becomes easy to hide."

That's what the financial lawyers had told me. I guess I should be glad my transactions would be done by the time Rio finished. Stopping her research and publication would be a motive for the kidnapping. "How close was she to finishing?"

"It is hard to tell with these things," Petr said. "Sometimes you feel like one breakthrough will answer all your questions, and sometimes the answer just adds more confusion. Rio would not talk about her work. No one does until it is published."

If he didn't know, how would I? One more step forward, but maybe only a half-step back. "Can we see where she worked?"

"Radim assures me that you have the need," Petr said. "Will you guarantee that her work is safe in your hands?"

So, Radim's word wasn't the key to all secrets. "I won't share what we see without Radim's approval. I probably won't understand it anyway."

Petr stood. "That will have to do. I think perhaps I was wrong. Rio is in trouble?"

"We don't know," I said.

Chapter 9

Petr took us to Rio's study room and unlocked the door. "Don't take anything away, please." He followed us in. "If it turns out that Rio is simply taking time out, I do not wish to explain how her research was disturbed."

If I showed him the picture of her, he wouldn't doubt it. But I couldn't trust what he would do with the information. For now, Rio had value for the kidnappers. Later... I didn't want to think about what would happen. "Can we have the key?" I asked. I didn't want to track him down every time we needed access.

"Of course." He handed it over.

"And a code to come in any time?" Restricting our access to only open hours might mean the difference between finding her and finding her body.

"I have everything," Radim said. He patted the pocket where he'd stored Rio's passwords.

"Do you need anything else from me?" Petr asked, checking his phone for the time. "I have a class."

I thanked him and let him leave. Radim held the door for me and then followed me inside. The room was larger than I expected. I guess the fees for a private university buy you space. Rio's desk sat at an angle in the corner across from the door, her chair behind the desk giving her a clear view of anyone who came in. Like an old-time gangster who insisted on facing the entry, Rio didn't like surprises.

A bookshelf took up most of the right wall, but print-outs covered the shelves, not reference books. In fact, not a textbook in sight. School had changed since I went, or it was possible criminal studies were stuck in the past and everything else evolved with technology.

No window, but the lights made up for the lack of sunlight. A soft yellow light was supplemented by a desk lamp and the glow from the monitor. Stained coffee cups and crumpled take-out bags filled the garbage bin and part of the floor.

The computer was just a monitor and a keyboard. I sat and tapped the space bar. The screen lit up with what I assumed was the school logo and a log-in box. "Pass-words?" I asked Radim.

He handed me the paper. There were four combina-tions of letters, numbers, and symbols. "Do you know which one is for this?" I gestured to the computer.

"My friend said she did not label them."

He should have told me that earlier. "So, these could be the passwords for her dating app?"

He laughed. "Let's see."

I entered the first two combinations and the universe must have been happy with me, because we were in.

There were only a few folders but each one was huge. I clicked on a document and it asked for a password. I typed in the next one on the list and the file opened. Rio was smart not to label her passwords, but not so smart by listing them in order.

The file was a template for a PhD thesis. It was blank.

The next file contained a series of links. I kept opening files until the entire folder was unlocked. Most of them needed one or the other of the passwords. "Nothing that says, 'here is the reason I was taken,'" Radim said.

I didn't appreciate his humor. "This is going to take forever."

"What are we looking for?" He maneuvered in beside me, making the corner feel even tighter.

"I hoped we'd know when we saw it." He leaned in to read the screen over my shoulder. I nudged him away. "That isn't helping."

"I know a friend who can help," he said, straightening up. "But she will need to understand what to look for."

"How many friends do you have?" I knew how hard it could be to make and keep contacts you could trust.

"I learned very young that times change, but people don't so much."

"That doesn't answer my question," I said, tired of his obscure comments about his history.

"To get more, you need to tell me something about your past," he said.

Okay, I had enough unimportant secrets to play his game. "I once betrayed my employer because they were defending a guilty client. They don't know. I don't think they care either – that I betrayed them, or that their client was guilty."

"When you live under different regimes, you learn that resistance is important, no matter who is in power."

His words shed a little light on him. I let my other questions go. Not because I wasn't interested, but because I didn't want to play tit for tat and let out my secret by mistake. I pulled out my phone and showed him the screenshot to avoid the conversation. "This guy was following Rio."

"When did you find this?" He expanded the picture. "Not enough detail for recognition."

"Last night," I said. "I was going to show you earlier, but you wanted to leave so fast."

"It's okay." He sent the picture to someone.

"Hey." I grabbed the phone back. "Don't do that without asking."

"I sent it to Petr. If the man is a student, he will tell us."

"I thought it more likely Jack sent a bodyguard. Rio is still a kid, after all." I checked the address on the text: Petr. So, he'd added the information to my contacts too. Was that a good sign, or just him taking control again?

"What did Jack say?"

My cheeks got warm. "I haven't asked him yet. He was too busy yelling at me to listen. I'll ask him later."

Petr's response came back. He didn't know the guy.

I leaned in and took a closer read of the folder names, thinking I would suddenly find a clue about how she organized her thoughts. I didn't. Radim leaned against the wall, watching me and making me nervous.

"Why don't you try looking through the printouts?" I said, pointing to the bookshelves.

"Why don't I go get us coffee?"

At least that would give me a little time alone with the files. "I like mine black," I said, focusing on the monitor.

When he left, I felt like someone had lifted a weight. I preferred working alone, but I had no idea how much until now. It scared me how I easily let someone else take the lead. Now that I was alone, ideas drifted in.

I opened all the folders and then the documents in them, thinking I'd find a word or link or something to help me grasp some meaning. The computer ground on my request for a few minutes, then hung. Not enough power. I expected the system to be more capable. I rebooted, re-entered the password and concentrated on the smallest folder.

These I could understand — a little. Articles on money laundering, ranging from PDFs of newspaper clippings to what appeared to me like confidential documents from governing agencies. Only a few were in English.

Radim came back with two paper cups. He placed mine on the desk; the coffee smelled delicious — espresso was the only way to go.

"So? Do I still need to go through those?" He nodded toward the bookshelf.

Time to start asking my own questions before my brain slid back into secondary mode. "What do you know about money laundering?" I was confident I'd found the basis of Rio's work, but knew there were a multitude of ways to slice out a PhD thesis.

"Criminals, terrorists, people who don't want their business public," he said.

"Criminals to clean money. They get pennies on the dollar," I said. "Is that the same for all of them?"

"Terrorists to mask where the donations come from to run their little gangs," he said as he joined me in the corner again. "Other people don't want to pay taxes and don't think of it as a crime. They buy and sell art and other things. Most of the work is the same as the criminal organizations, but not so hard on the victims."

Pretty much what I knew. "I wonder which one Rio stumbled on?"

He rested against the wall as if he could tell I needed the space. "You are certain they took her for this?"

"I don't know, but my gut says it can't be unrelated." I pointed at the list of articles. "Why would she keep this if it wasn't part of her research? And Petr said she was looking at the flow of money. You wouldn't do that for legitimate funds."

"Can we go by your gut? Maybe she is looking for hints for the next crisis."

Focusing on money laundering was a risk. If I was wrong, Rio could suffer. Why did I feel this so strongly? "We know it's about data flow. These days, money is data, right? Transactions are tracked, but so many that it's hard to separate the legitimate from the criminal."

He tossed his empty cup into the garbage can. "It would be helpful if we could tell the police how to sort through all the mess."

"And she was sure her result would help the police," I finished his thought. "Am I only seeing what I think supports my guess?"

"Look more. Try to prove the opposite. Time I started helping." He moved to the bookshelves, placed all the printouts on the floor, and settled next to them, picking up the first one.

"This would be easier if we had more chairs and a table," I said. I wasn't going to offer to switch places, but I did feel sympathy; the rug was thin, and the floor covered in tile.

"Too much to smuggle in," he said.

I clicked open another article. It looked like a blueprint for a storage facility at first glance. Then I read some of the labels. I grabbed my phone and searched for the words. "She has the schematic for a bank's data warehouse," I said. "I don't think they'd want the plan public."

"Perhaps we have friends in common," Radim said. "Maybe not. This is a university. Students are willing to break a few laws to get what they want, yes? Hackers learn from somewhere."

"Hacking supports the idea that she was working on

money laundering because none of that is public information. I don't know how she thought she could use it if hacking formed part of the research. How would she cite the source? If she just got the schematic, it could be the reason they took her now."

"Let's hope we get a chance to ask her," he said.

I took my attention away from the screen to see him flipping through an inch-thick printout. "Find anything?"

"Her notes on the things you are finding, I think," he said. "She was cautious enough not to create paper copies of what she stole."

I thought stealing was a bit harsh. But maybe that's how people end up as criminals — start with a gray area and the next thing you know, you're working in the darker side of life. When I met Rio at the company party, she struck me as less idealistic and more practical; that didn't guarantee she'd be safeguarded against bad decisions.

"Your friend," I said. "The one you said might help us. I think we know enough to give her some direction. You said she is the best."

He glanced up from the pile of papers. "This is too dangerous for her," he said. "I have another friend, one who can take care of herself if she's caught."

I wondered why he told me that. Was he warning me about the danger? It wasn't a conversation we needed to get into right now. I checked my phone. Three texts and two missed calls from Jack.

I opened his texts. If we required proof that he was frantic about his daughter, the first two messages would be enough — if you didn't know Jack. I couldn't shake the feeling that all this was for show. It didn't matter, of course; Rio was still in trouble and I had to help.

The third text was another photo. "Radim," I said, moving out from behind the desk.

He turned away from the printouts. When he saw the screen, he swore. I thought I could hide my emotions, but the picture on my screen was hard to take. I wouldn't have recognized her if I didn't see the tattoo. She'd been beaten badly, and they wanted it to show. Flashes of pain and nausea surged back from five years ago when I had lost a fight. The bruises had taken weeks to finally fade, the memory as fresh as if it was me in the picture. Rio was still alive, and I had to concentrate on that.

Everything was swollen; her left eye just a line in the middle of dark bulge, her mouth distorted, her lips bleeding. On the right side there were cuts that could have been the result of a hard punch.

She was still tied to the chair, this time slumped to the left. Whatever the damage to her side, they hid it under her clothes. If it wasn't for the right eye, I would have thought she was dead. But she stared at the camera like she was memorizing the person holding it and making plans for revenge. I checked the time code on the picture: two hours ago.

I'd done damage to a source in my last case. I don't remember where the anger came from that drove me to beat him until he told me what I needed. I do remember he hadn't been this bad when I finished.

Her glare and the extent of the injuries scared me. If they didn't care about how she looked, it meant Rio couldn't go out in public anytime soon without raising questions. The only good thing about this was that they couldn't move her until dark, so no one would see her.

"If we can find where she is, we could rescue her before any ransom demand," I said. It sounded inane, but anything else would have ended with me screaming obscenities or crying.

Radim touched my shoulder and the contact helped ground the fury.

"I have an idea." He called someone and spoke quietly in Czech.

I kept staring at the picture, trying to keep my eyes on the details around her, but drawn to the pain and wrath I could see looking back at me.

"There's some tile work," I said. "No windows." The photo was better than the last one, which might have been taken at another location. The kidnappers needed the bright light to make their point clear. Rio meant nothing to them but what she could be sold for.

Radim pointed to my phone and held out his hand. I passed it over reluctantly. I felt like I was giving him Rio.

He tapped the picture and forwarded it to another number, then ended his call.

Another text came through, pushing the image up the screen. Jack ordering me to phone him.

"I don't suppose you recognized anything in the background," I said, ignoring Jack.

"Tiles are common. I think it's an abandoned building, but there are many here. My friend will let us know quickly if there is any way to find that particular place."

My successes with tracing texts was spotty. Mostly because hackers didn't see it as a challenge. Either they told me no right away, or the job went on a back burner. But I'd never asked for this kind of trace.

Jack sent another text.

"I guess I should call him," I said.

Chapter 10

I sat before I connected with Jack because I was still reeling with anger and echoes of pain; sitting felt like it might be calming.

"Nice of you to bother calling," he said.

"What did the kidnappers want?" I ignored his tone. It was one AM in Vancouver, I pretended to believe that made a difference.

"Nothing," he said. "Still no ransom. Why isn't she safe yet?"

Radim was watching me and that was the main reason I kept my temper. The other reason was it would have no effect on Jack. No matter how much I asked him to let me work the case, he wouldn't stop interfering. "Why did they contact you?"

"I asked for proof of life," he said. This time there was pain in his voice.

"You called them?" If he had a number for these assholes and kept it to himself, I'd toss this phone and buy a new one just to stop him calling.

"No. Obviously if I had a way to contact them, I

would be hunting them down with someone more competent than you."

I paused for a breath. Reacting to his comments would just escalate the fight. And he wasn't listening to what he was saying. Jack was a father desperate to save his daughter. If I could keep reminding myself of that then we might work better together. "When did you ask to see her alive?"

"When they sent the first text," he said. "I didn't know if the first picture was old, if she was killed right after, or what they'd done with her. If Rio dies, I don't want to waste time trying to play their game."

"And what game are they playing?" I asked. "It sounds like you think this is about more than some ransom."

"Nothing to do with you," he said. "Just find Rio and get her away from them."

Knowing about her studies didn't feel like much of a breakthrough now that I was thinking of telling Jack. "What do you know about what Rio's studies?"

Radim looked up from his phone and moved closer. He held it up to show me the contents of the text — actually in English this time.

Date stamp seems legitimate. No location information in metadata. Might be stripped.

"Ever since she was a kid, Rio's been smarter than her friends. Now, in her field, she's too smart to dumb it down for me. The school says she's a couple of years ahead of their expectations. Their best advice was to connect her with people in research or some related field so she'd have someone to talk with on her level."

Good to know I wasn't the only one who didn't understand this stuff. "Why would they tell you that? Isn't Rio's future up to her?"

"Her brilliance doesn't extend to the real world," Jack

sneered the words out. "If she could, Rio would spend her life studying."

"I have some updates," I said, trying to stave off the next comment. Every word chipped away at my hope Jack actually cared about Rio as a person rather than as an asset.

"When were you going to report?"

I let silence fill the space while I controlled my urge to yell at him about having time to work between calls and texts.

"What did you find?" His voice was calmer.

"First, the picture was taken this morning. I had someone do the analysis. They couldn't find a location, but she was alive a couple of hours ago."

"I assigned people to look into that too," he said.

"And you were going to tell me when?"

"If you paid attention to my calls, you wouldn't be falling behind, and my daughter would be safe," Jack said. "What else?"

"She was taken from outside the university. I think it has something to do with her studies."

"They should have kept her safe," Jack said. "They won't get another penny from me."

"Don't do anything right now, Jack. You want to keep this quiet, right? If you complain to the people who run the university, you'll lose any chance of keeping this secret."

This time he held off on speaking. I was happy to be patient.

Finally, he sighed deeply. "I wasn't thinking," he said. "Send me her research and I'll have someone look into it."

Normally that would be the right thing. At home his 'someone' would be my contact. Here, there was no way I would let Jack cause more problems. "I already have someone sorting through the data." I looked at Radim for confirmation. He lifted his chin. I didn't know whether he meant yes, or soon, or maybe not.

"It would be better for two sets of eyes to look into it." Not an argument; not acceptance either. He wasn't letting the subject go.

"There's no way to send this anyway," I said, making up what I hoped was a believable excuse. "It's too big and the university firewall won't let someone outside log in."

"I thought you didn't have any contacts," Jack said. "How are you accessing the expertise you need?"

All business now. "As you said yesterday, I'm good at making connections."

Radim grinned at my response. He'd moved away and was standing in the door, looking at his phone.

"How do you think her work is related to this?" Jack asked.

"I don't know yet," I said. "I need to ask you a couple of questions."

"What?"

"Are you paying for a bodyguard?"

"Why do you think that?"

"Someone was following her. Are you?"

"What makes you think so?"

I wasn't going to tell him we'd accessed the accounts. "I don't think it. I hope."

"No."

If I sent him the photo, he'd use it as another angle to obstruct our progress, such as it was. "I have to go. Don't text or call unless the kidnappers make contact."

"You work for me," Jack said, halfheartedly.

"No. I don't anymore, remember? This is the last thing I'm doing for the firm. In fact, I'm not investigating for the firm. This is all for Rio. You're only footing the bill."

"Don't cut me out, Sharka," Jack said. "I won't just sit and wait for you to call. Rio is my daughter. I want her back."

"Goodbye, Jack."

Radim joined me back at the computer. "How can you be sure we can't get into the system from outside?"

"I'm not. I needed him to believe we can't. There's definitely too much here to send to him." I was a little impressed with myself that Radim had believed me.

"We should make sure you're right," he said. "If this is about her studies, we lose our chance if they log in and take this."

"I wonder why they haven't done it." The possibility worried me. I hadn't thought about the kidnappers doing the same as we were, another indication that my mind needed rest. "We should change the codes."

"That might be bad for Rio."

"If they haven't tried by now, I don't think it will matter," I said. "Something about this whole thing is wrong."

"Tell me." He sat on the edge of the desk, slipped his phone into his pocket, and gave me his full attention.

"I've done enough investigations to develop an instinct for things," I said. Having to voice my concerns made me think more deeply about what I was feeling. "Saving kidnap victims is new to me," I said. "But I've seen parents react to devastating news about their kids. Kids who made one bad decision that turned into a life sentence."

"Jack is not behaving properly?"

He boiled it down to the core without thinking too hard. "Is there a right way to act when faced with this?"

"Like you, I've seen parents face the consequences of a child's choices. They are all different, but also all the same. They only care about what they can do to save the child."

"Jack isn't doing that," I said. "Did you hear him?"

I hadn't put the phone on speaker when Jack called because he'd know someone else was listening. Telling him about Radim didn't seem like a smart idea. He would use us against each other.

"No, only what you said. He argues with you about the wrong things. He wants control. He blames you for something."

That was a new interpretation. "He's setting me up," I said. "If I don't find Rio, he'll make me responsible somehow. But to who?"

"Why did you agree to do this?"

"Rio is just a kid, I couldn't refuse to help," I said.

"I don't believe it was only that."

I didn't want to tell him anything, but he needed to know. "Jack has something on me."

"So, he is blackmailing you to find his daughter? Maybe I can make your problem go away?"

My mouth opened to say my first reaction. Then I thought. Radim might not be able to do it without leaving a trail, and it's always the cover-up that causes the worst problem. As much as I wanted to be free, at least I knew where I stood with Jack. Radim might be worse. "No need, I handled it. Believe me, I wouldn't have left her to the kidnappers," I said. "And I'm not sure that's what Jack is forcing me to do."

Radim smiled. "Nothing is only one thing."

"He's putting more pressure on me to find out why she was taken, and what she might know, than on finding her." I missed that in all the nastiness.

"So, we don't trust him. We tell him as close to nothing as possible. Unless you want to stop."

"You saw that picture. If I walk away, I would be responsible if... who am I kidding, *when* she dies."

"Good. Then Jack only hears our progress in finding Rio, nothing about why or what," Radim said.

"I'm not sure they can be kept separate," I said as I turned back to the computer.

"On this we agree. But that doesn't mean we tell Jack what we find. And a lie or two won't hurt when we find her."

I laughed, catching his optimism. "Now it's starting to sound like something I'm happy to do." I changed the password and logged off. "We need to do something more," I said.

"We don't want to alert them that we're looking."

I couldn't just sit and wait. "Maybe I can get us something." I leaned my butt against the desk; standing felt more like I was doing something and sitting made my body think it was okay to take a nap.

I sent a text to Michael, asking him to call me. It was too early in the morning to hope for an answer; by my calculations, it was around two. Even if I had to wait a few hours, I wanted his take on Jack's behavior. I knew how risky it was to let my own suspicions run the case. I'd wasted enough time when I started out as an investigator chasing down rabbit holes leading nowhere. Maybe Jack was really distressed at Rio's situation. Maybe he was trying — unsuccessfully — to hold himself together.

"We must wait here for a little longer." He stretched his arms over his head and yawned. "I want to move on, too. My friend will be here to go through the work. She said she can hack into the system, but it would take time, so I invited her to come to us."

"Are you sure we can leave her with this?" A big part of me wanted to just trust his contact, but if she did something to Rio's files, it might end in her death. Or mine if we rescued Rio and her PhD research was screwed up.

"Yes," he said. "She has done this for me before. She can be trusted."

"I need a little more than that. How do you know? Have you needed to analyze academic studies before?"

"No. It is not important what she did. She proved to me she is trustworthy. When she comes, we'll get her to work and then we can go."

"So, if I trust you, then I trust all your contacts?"

"You are starting at the wrong place. If you trust Michael, then you trust me and my contacts."

Before I could argue back, my phone rang. Speak of the devil. "Pulling an all-nighter, Michael?"

"I can't exactly do the work you need at the office, and I can't call in sick much more." When he worked private jobs, Michael suddenly came down with the flu.

"Good thing you're excellent at your job," I said. "If you've been away from work, I guess you don't know what Jack's been doing."

"I stayed most of the day. When my searches came in, I left. Are you saying the firm needs some distance from this?"

"Probably. Look, I can't get a handle on the way Jack is behaving. What's going on at the office?" I rubbed my eyes, the remnants of jet lag reminding me that at home everyone would be asleep.

"He's acting like Jack," Michael said. "Is Radim there?"

"I'll put you on speaker." I tapped the icon. "Go ahead."

"He's getting texts from all kinds of phones in Europe. Never the same one twice. Some in Germany, some in Greece, some in the Czech Republic."

"Clients as well as the kidnappers?" It didn't help to wipe away my feeling that Jack was hiding something.

"I can't tell without the contents."

"They are probably all from here, in Prague," Radim said. "The networks are all linked. Unless his clients use burner phones?"

"I wouldn't be surprised," I said. "How untraceable are they? Can you find out who sent them?"

"I'm still working on it," Michael said. "I might have the content of the texts soon."

"Would it be better if we did the tracking from here?" I asked.

"Maybe.Not because it will be easier to do, but because you can act on it faster. Let me figure out how to send you the details. Radim, I assume you still have a lot of friends?"

"I am careful to keep them close," Radim said. "I have someone in mind."

"Anything else?" Michael asked.

There was no way I could ask about trusting Radim. "Keep an eye on Jack and give me a heads-up if he's planning to join us," I said. "His texts and calls are bad enough. If he comes over, I don't think we'll get anything else done."

"I could put his name on the no-fly list." Michael laughed when he said it, but I had no doubt he could do that and more.

"Probably overkill," I said. "Just a heads-up will do. Get some sleep."

"I could say the same to you," Michael said. The call ended.

Chapter 11

So now we were just waiting around. Knowing we had nothing to follow up on didn't make me feel less helpless. At least when I was talking to Michael, I had something to do.

"How long until your friend with the computer skills arrives?"

"Soon," Radim said. "Where do we go from here?"

It was disconcerting to hear him ask. Until now, Radim had seemed in charge, something I'd fought against without a real alternative plan. "I haven't a clue."

"It's not good that we are stuck waiting," he said. "Today seems like everything is hidden in little electronic rooms. But I don't know if we are looking in the right place."

"It's been that way most of my career," I said. "Use information to find someone who will talk. That hasn't changed. Somewhere we'll find a person. No matter how much hacking we do, the weak link is always a human being." Being familiar with the feeling didn't make it any less frustrating.

"Rio didn't leave any names in the printouts," Radim said. "For me, it's better to find the weak link fast. I know every hack leaves a trail to be followed back. This is a race to find what we want before the villains do."

"Isn't it always that way?"

"When the secrets were kept in files, or on recordings, it was easy to find someone who could be bribed, black-mailed, or beaten to reveal them."

I wondered if he'd been on both sides of those scenarios. "Computers can't be bribed, or blackmailed. Beating them is worse than useless."

"When Maura arrives, perhaps she'll find something we can act on," Radim said.

"And if she doesn't? Or needs more time?"

"You said the kidnappers didn't ask for a ransom."

"That's what Jack told me."

"So, I suggest we eat lunch."

As much as I wanted to rush around doing something, or feel like I was, we needed a lead. "What if more than one hacker was working on the files?"

"No."

"No, you won't bring in someone else? Or no, it wouldn't work?" I could always ask Michael for another contact here, one with the skills.

"They are not what you call team players."

He was still holding onto nothing more than a few words. A reasoned debate might be asking too much, but these were no different from one-word answers.

"They will compete to find the information," I said. "Two points of view might reveal something more."

"They will compete, yes. To find answers, maybe not. They hack to win, and they will define win."

"How do you know?" What about hacker groups like

Anonymous? They worked together to expose all sorts of secrets.

"You are thinking of the collectives, yes? The ones who make the news? They work for their own agenda. They make more mistakes than people hear about. You know that, I think."

"The medical records?" I could sense my idea fading into obscurity.

"That and others they kept quiet. We use professionals, not idealists."

"Fine."

I stopped arguing. Maybe food would help me think. And maybe I was fighting the wrong battle with Radim.

Twenty minutes later Maura rolled in. Her wheelchair was black, at least that seemed to be the unifying color. The chair was wrapped in bright straps with beads and glitter. Whatever she did for people like Radim, she wasn't part of some shadowy underground. Her hair was pink and spiked. She was wearing a black tank top and jeans. Her nose, lips, and eyebrows were pierced, and her skin was covered in the kind of tattoos Popeye might have coveted.

"Move the desk and get rid of that *shite* chair," she rasped in an Irish accent.

I helped Radim pull the desk to the center of the room. He lifted the chair to me, and we moved to the tiny space left near the bookshelves. Maura had room to maneuver, but we were cramped. It made me want to go outside even more.

"Passwords," she said.

I gave them to her. "Tell me if you need to change them," I said. "Rio will need to get back into her files when she's—"

Maura flicked her hand at me. "I don't care. I'll text

the new ones to Radim if I need to change them. What am I looking for?"

I looked to Radim to explain, afraid to violate her boundaries by giving too much detail about Rio. He spoke in English. I guess I should be grateful.

He gestured to the computer and the printouts. "This might tell us why a girl was kidnapped. You're looking for something to prove that."

"Or prove you wrong," Maura said. "No prejudgment."

"If you can't find a link, we need to know quickly," I said. "She's—"

"I don't care if she's the Virgin Mary reborn. It'll take what it takes. Go get me some coffee or a beer or something."

Radim took my arm and pulled me into the hall. "Half an hour," he said. "Time enough for her to learn if something is there, not the meaning, or how it will help, but that will be enough for now."

This is what the lawyers must have felt when they sent me to find dirt on the other side and then had to let me take over. I'd given the speech to Jack multiple times over the last twenty hours. Knowing Radim was right didn't make it easier to leave.

"There's a place across the way," I said. Costa Coffee was like Starbucks here; one on every corner.

"Too fast," Radim said, steering me away from the main street and around to the side door where Rio had been taken.

In the daylight, the street didn't seem so perfect for crime. Tourists followed guides who told them interesting but probably not accurate stories. The shops were open, and sunlight cast a warm glow on the forbidding, windowless wall of the university.

"You think we'll find something here now?" I didn't think any evidence could survive this long.

"Let's see if anyone opens the door," he said.

We approached the side door of the university. Radim banged on the wood and waited. It only took moments for someone to answer his knock. The door swung open to reveal a security guard. "No entrance," he said.

Radim spoke to him in Czech. He answered. I felt like no one knew I was part of anything.

They finished talking, the door closed. Radim nodded across the street. "Coffee."

The tiny store was next to the bank. I briefly wondered if we could gain entrance there and ask to see all the security footage. We had no credentials; we'd more likely close a door than open one, so I didn't suggest it.

"Three espresso," Radim said to the young woman behind the counter.

"Right away," she said. A fellow Canadian by the accent, Nova Scotia.

"You know anything about the students?" I asked.

"Rich kids," she said. "They come and go. They don't notice anyone not wearing designer clothes."

Rio wasn't like that, but there was no use arguing with this girl. "What about next door?"

Radim gave me a side glance. I ignored the look. He could have told me what the security guard said, but he didn't. At least he could understand what I was saying so he could express an opinion.

"Richer. Mostly men with bodyguards," she said. "Not much activity. Why?"

"She is just curious," Radim said. "You know how tourists can be. They think everything they see is something to photograph or blog about."

The girl rolled her eyes as if she wasn't from elsewhere.

She put the paper cups in a cardboard tray and passed it to Radim, printed the bill and handed the slip to me. I paid with Euros, crumpled the receipt and followed Radim from the store.

"Okay, what happened with the security guard?" I asked him.

"He said most of the students leave by the side door when they are late because no one knows. Going out the front means they must find someone to lock the door, but here it just locks behind them."

"That seems odd," I said. "Why would the university use different locks on the doors?"

He handed me one of the cups as we crossed the fore-court to the front doors. "Rules. Buildings like this must not be changed." He pulled open the door and pointed at the lock. "See? They would have to drill through to add security."

When I pushed the door to Rio's study room, music assaulted my body. The rooms must be soundproofed because there had been no indication of the head-banging metal screams Maura was playing.

She looked up from behind the monitor. The raucous noise died, and she held out her hand for the coffee. "No pastry? You cheap bastard."

"You've found something," Radim said.

"How do you know that?" Maura opened two pack-ages of sugar and stirred the coffee.

"You are too cheerful," he said. "What is it?"

"The data," Maura said. She sipped the espresso. "Damn. Good coffee is almost better than whiskey. I don't have any details, yet. I will though. It's pretty clear she was following a huge global money laundering scheme."

"Just following?" Rio might have made a mistake and

no matter what we did, she was going to die. "Would they know?"

"How the *feck* should I know?" Maura said. "Now get out and let me play. I'll text you if I find anything specific."

"Now we eat," Radim said. "And we talk."

We headed toward Wenceslas square. The crowds were getting thicker, meaning it was harder to hear. I grabbed his arm, he stopped.

"We can't talk about this in public," I said. "I'm not going to sit around waiting for food. Rio is in real trouble."

He put his hands on my shoulders. "Yes, she is in more than we thought. But she's still kidnapped, and we still don't know where to look."

"And you think talking where we can be overheard is a good idea? We don't know if we're being followed. We need to do something."

I wasn't panicking, no matter what I sounded like. Up until now, I'd been convinced this was about Jack. Either he'd crossed the wrong person, or someone targeted Rio just because he was rich and could pay a ransom. I hung on the hope that Rio had a chance, even a small one, of living through this. But if she triggered the kidnapping by catching the attention of the kind of people who controlled that much money, this wasn't about Jack. Or more likely, they thought he knew something about what Rio was doing. Whoever took her had wanted information and control over it. Their ransom request would be in something other than cash.

"We can't trust anything we've learned up to now," I said.

"Yes. But I am used to that," Radim said. "You have the option of going to the police. I know someone in Interpol who would listen, if that is what you want."

"Of course, you do," I said.

Now terror was spiraling, killing any chance of rational thought. I took a deep breath, holding onto Radim so he couldn't walk away. Then I looked around. Despite my fear of being overheard, the crowd didn't pay attention to us. Most of them were so intent on following their guide, they didn't even step around us until they realized we weren't moving. This was probably the safest place to talk. Once again, Radim was better at this than me. Until I came here, I thought my life was shady and I was able to handle anything. Stupid and naive.

Radim removed my hand from his arm. "So, do I call him?"

One more breath and I won the battle with fear. "No. Not yet," I said. I wouldn't risk Rio's life, but right now we weren't that far along and if the cops came into the search, we'd be sidelined. "We keep going until we know for sure."

"I hope that is the right decision," he said. "Michael asked me to help you, and I will, but not to your death, Sharka. If I think you are taking too many risks, I will call my Interpol contact without asking you."

Chapter 12

"I'm not hungry," I said.

"Okay, we go for a beer," Radim said. "Until Maura finds a thread for us to pull, we can maybe come up with some ideas."

I wasn't sure about the beer, but if it got me out of the press of bodies and somewhere we had the peace to think, I'd be happy. "Where?"

He turned around and led me away from the crowd. I was certain we were heading in the direction of last night's pub. A good place to stop unless more customers came in the afternoon than late at night.

He led me to a bookstore, The Globe. We walked through to the back and sat at a table on the patio. Only two other people occupied a table outside, and they bent over laptops; perhaps coffee shop working or studying was a global habit.

We sat in the far corner; he ordered beer.

"Water, too, please." I shucked my jacket and looked around. The space was basically a courtyard. The walls were the sides of buildings, windows and tiny balconies looked down on us. I felt sheltered and completely separate from the city outside.

When our beers and water arrived, we were left alone by the waiter.

I poured and drank two glasses of the water so I wouldn't slake my thirst with beer.

"What do we do next?" Radim asked.

It was nice that he didn't try to win me around to his idea of calling the police. "Now we know what it's really about, we might figure out who would want the information Rio gathered."

"You think she was trying to take the money?"

I sipped my beer while I thought about my answer. "I'm not familiar enough with Rio to be sure," I said finally. "You saw her studies. Do you think she planned to steal money?"

"I think she was more interested in finding the answers than taking money." He'd already drunk the first pint. The waiter came with a fresh one. "The room was practical. Her father would give her money for what she wanted?"

"I think Jack would prefer she show off her riches," I said. "I only met her a few times. She was wearing basic clothes, not designer. Everything seemed planned to piss her father off. The tattoo and piercing formed a similar tactic, even if she thought otherwise. Her attitude isn't likely to change while she's still basically a kid. I'm not sure it will ever change."

"Where does she live?"

"I'm an idiot." Shit, why hadn't I asked Jack that? My cheeks were burning and not because of the beer. Was I so worried about my future I'd screwed up? I sent a text to Jack asking for the information.

Radim tipped his head. "Because you didn't ask him? I think he should have given every piece of information to you without asking. Don't take on more than your share of guilt."

"When he answers, we'll check her place," I said. Radim's comments didn't stop me berating myself. I was a professional. You don't turn that off. "So why did they take her from here? And why now?"

"She was here," Radim said.

"Yes, but they kept her in Prague as far as we know. Who is the big criminal boss around here? There must be someone." We'd see how extensive his network was.

He grinned at me. "You plan to march into a crime boss's home and demand he tell you where the girl is?"

I couldn't blame him for the patronizing attitude. So far, I had screwed up the basics. "I'm not stupid enough to do that," I said. "But maybe we can get close. You have a lot of friends. You must know the players."

"No one I know is important enough to challenge a man like that. Those people tend to be dangerous as friends or enemies. They only collect favors, never owe them."

"But we are going to need to deal with them sometime," I said. "How close can you get me?"

"We must be cautious," he said. "Maura will tell us what we need so I can find the right person."

I checked my phone. No response from Jack and that was worrying given his previous behavior. "Maura kicked us out before, but do you think you could check with her?"

"You saw who she is," he said. "Maura won't answer until she is sure."

"So, you don't want to be like Jack?" I asked. "Waiting is hard."

I finished my beer and tried to call Jack. It was still only four AM in Vancouver. I got his voicemail. "Maybe he's asleep," I said. "We need someone who runs with the kind of people who would take her." Radim's concerns had some value, but we were getting nowhere trying to stay safe.

"I know of someone," Radim said into his glass. "He's a bad guy."

"So, what are we looking for here?" I asked. "I appreciate that you don't want to make this more dangerous than it already is, but Rio needs our help. I don't think we will do that without talking to dangerous people."

"I'm not sure you understand what the word dangerous really means. Here, things are different." He continued to stare at his beer.

He usually met my eyes. He wasn't avoiding me because he didn't think I could take whatever came at me. I wanted to believe he was worried about both of us because if it was just me, I'd be pissed.

"Bad guys are bad guys. How can he be worse than people traffickers, or drug dealers, or anything else criminals get involved in?" I kept my voice light, fighting with him wouldn't gain me any advantage right now. I'd seen this before in other cases. Radim needed me to convince him, not bully him.

I waited for him to answer me. My confidence that I would be able to handle anything waned as the seconds ticked past. What could be worse than what I'd encountered so far?

After a few minutes of silence, Radim looked up at me again. "The history of my country has made people do things that stain them with shame. Some of them move on, as you say. They put the past behind them and become good citizens. Become businessmen. Become bankers. Become teachers. But some of them... For some people, once they make the first step into violence, they can't come back."

Which group was he in? I couldn't imagine him becoming one of those people who couldn't turn back. But despite what I did for a living, I realized I was sheltered in Canada. I had never been through anything like Europeans had in the last century, and the Czech people had been through more than most European countries. I guess they needed longer to heal.

I didn't know what to ask to make him talk about his past. So, I just focused on the case. "The people who took Rio aren't standing in the sunshine, Radim. We're more likely to find out where she is, or why she was taken, or even who took her, by talking to the very people you don't want me to meet."

"Yes. I see that. I will try to set up a meeting. This person only works at night. So, we still have today to search for what we need. I hope we don't need to resort to owing a favor to someone who won't ask you to take his dog for a walk."

"Maybe we can pass the favor along to Jack. It would be more valuable to have a lawyer owe you something in this person's line of work, than one of us owe him, or even both of us."

Radim pulled out his phone and sent a text. "When we meet, allow me to do everything. You don't like that, it's been obvious all day. This man takes offense very easily and I know him well enough to avoid insulting him."

"I can't guarantee I'll keep my mouth shut," I said. "I'll do my best."

"He is very charming," Radim said. He glanced at the screen again, then put it down beside him on the table. "Do not let his charm trick you into believing he's harmless."

I'd read that psychopaths can be charismatic. Although

I'd never met one, as far as I knew. Charm didn't make me do anything I wouldn't do otherwise.

My phone pinged.

It was the first time Jack had actually given us some help. His silence over the last couple of hours made it seem like he'd been sulking. The text contained Rio's address. Jack said he'd been sleeping. I guess exhaustion was understandable, if he was grieving Rio that much. Although grief was probably a little premature.

WE GOT access to her building pretty easily. A woman was leaving with a dog on a leash. She didn't pay attention when Radim caught the door before it closed. There was no elevator, but at least Rio didn't live on the 10th floor. There were only three and she was on the top, so I counted my blessings.

From outside, the building looked big enough to hold two or three apartments on each floor, but we didn't pass any people, and each corridor had a fire door closing it off from the stairwell. As we climbed the final flight of stairs, the door on the right opened and a man stepped out. He acted surprised to find us on the stairs, but in the kind of 'okay, I wasn't expecting anybody' startle rather than anything indicating he was suspicious about us. We nodded a greeting as he passed.

Radim opened the fire door and I followed through. There were two apartments on this side of the building. Rio's was on the left. There was just a regular key lock. I tried the knob, hoping we'd be lucky and the door would be unlocked. But of course, it was locked. Radim slipped a credit card between the door and the jam, and the door clicked open. I thought Rio would've had better security on her home, but perhaps she hadn't cared.

The door opened into a short dim corridor. There was no light switch. I'm not sure how the chandelier that hung halfway down got turned on, but enough light came from the windows ahead of us to show the way.

I don't know what I expected when I stepped into the space, but it wasn't the mess confronting me. Every piece of furniture, except the heavy couch, was tossed, a couple of them broken. She had a few books and ornaments which had started out on shelving. Those lay on the floor, and the shelves had been pulled out of the brackets and dropped on top of the rubble. Someone had sliced the cushions on the couch, as if thinking she had somehow stuffed some secrets inside.

I left Radim in the living room and moved into the tiny kitchen; everything had been spilled out of the cupboards onto the counter and floor. A pool of milk soaked into a dusting of flour. It was still wet.

"This was done recently," I called back to Radim.

I stepped into the living room. He wasn't there. I checked the bathroom quickly. The shower curtain was slashed. Some of her beauty products were dumped into the sink, but there wasn't much in the room to cause a lot of damage.

"He is gone," Radim said as he joined me in the back in the living room. "The man we passed. He must've done this."

"Yeah. This was only done a few minutes ago. I'm not sure how long he was here. And I can't be sure if he found anything. You think Jack sent someone else?"

"To do this much damage? We should still look," Radim said. "We don't know if he was in a hurry. We didn't interrupt him. He was finished with his search. What else can we do?"

It sounded so hopeless, possibly because of the mental

filter I applied as I heard his words. "I think if we try to tidy up a bit, it might help us decide on where to keep looking. Right now, this just looks like a giant mess and I can't find a starting place."

Radim started righting the furniture, as much as he could. A chair and a side table had broken legs, so he stacked them in the kitchen. It didn't help a lot, but they had been hiding the mess on the floor that included one of those wireless assistants. Alexa, or Cortana, or one I never heard of. I wish I had gloves to protect my fingerprints. The police might need to search through this, and I would prefer my involvement in this not be obvious.

Radim pulled a pair leather gloves out of his pocket and slipped them on. I guess he may have had more reason to hide his presence than I did. I nodded towards the device. "Let's find out if that works."

The case was cracked, but I could still see the logo. "Alexa, turn on the lights." It wasn't much, but we knew immediately she was working when the chandelier in the hallway turned on.

"Do you know how to work this?" Radim asked. "What else will it do for us?"

"No. If we had a password for her, we could find out. Maybe the guy who ransacked the place didn't know how to turn her on?"

I tried a few more commands. She wouldn't turn on the TV, but perhaps that's because a crack shattered the screen, and it was lying on the floor. She also didn't respond to the same login codes Rio had used at the university. So even if she had the answers we needed, we weren't going to get them.

"Why would they search her apartment like this? They must know who she is. They know who Jack is. This isn't going to get them money." I checked the couch cushions, squeezing the corners to see if perhaps the guy had missed something.

"They wouldn't." Radim was moving things to clear the floor. And then tapping on the hardwood. That was a good idea. Perhaps Rio hid something under the boards.

I bent down to join him. "So, we agree? This is about the information, not money, right?"

"Yes. This is not about the money," Radim said. "We have nothing to say she has any other secrets. And, if Maura is right about what she was searching for, or if we are right about what she found in those files, I think we can be pretty sure it's about her research."

Being pretty sure about something didn't help us take the next steps. I had to admit it did feel a little like progress though.

By the time we finished clearing the floor, well, really just moving around the mess so we could test the sections of the boards for hollow sounds, it was clear to me that if Rio had hidden something inside her apartment, it wasn't something that could be held in a secret safe.

Radim went to the kitchen and came back with a plastic bag.

"Will that thing work if we take it away from her home?"

I was not an expert on these devices, but I knew they worked on a WiFi system, so maybe she could be hooked up to another one. "I'm sure you have a friend who can work with her." I didn't mean to sound sarcastic, but Radim gave me a look that told me I came across that way. "I mean, seriously, you have a friend for everything."

"I will need to find out if any of my contacts know about these things."

Now that we knew this wasn't about money, I hoped Jack would be more helpful. "I'm going to call Jack," I said. "I have a feeling he knows more about this than he's said so far."

"When he says there has been no ransom call, do you think he's lying?" Radim tucked a few more objects in the bag along with the Echo. "That he knows what they want, and he is certain they won't be asking for money?"

"I hope not. What kind of father would hold back any information that would free his daughter when she's been beaten so badly? Wouldn't you be giving everything you could to bring your daughter back?"

Some pain crossed Radim's face. He breathed in and then said, "Remember what I said about people crossing a line? How well do you know Jack?"

It was a good question.

Jack didn't answer his phone. I sent him a text, hoping to provoke him to call me. Hoping he wasn't still sulking. Hoping he wasn't doing something to make things harder for us.

"Do you think she only used electronics?"

Radim's question kind of brought me back to the room. I had no idea of the answer. I looked at him and he was holding a notebook.

"Where did you find that?"

"Under the couch," he said. "We're lucky he didn't turn it over." He handed the book to me.

I opened it and saw names and numbers. "Contacts? Friends? Something to help us finally."

Radim took the notebook and added it to the bag. I reached in and pulled it out. "We need to call these people," I said.

"We can do that from a restaurant," Radim said. "I know you want to act on this but look at your hand."

I didn't have to do that to understand what he was talking about. My hand was shaking, and I had the cold sensation I get if I don't eat for hours. My brain knew it was late afternoon and I'd eaten breakfast hours ago. Not paying attention to my body had already affected the case. If I hadn't been so exhausted, I'd have thought to ask for Rio's address right at the beginning. And we wouldn't be standing in this landfill of an apartment because we would have beaten whoever made the mess. And we might already have found Rio.

"Okay, but we need to be quick." I handed Radim the notebook to add to the contents of his bag.

Radim led me down a narrow street to a small restaurant. There were a few tables inside and a loft with more. Radim talked to the waiter — probably another friend — and we got a seat by the door.

"You like pizza?"

"Who doesn't?" It would be fast, and I could eat it and make calls.

He ordered after asking me what I liked. A bottle of water arrived in moments, making me realize hunger wasn't my only problem. I poured and then asked for the notebook.

Radim handed it over, then pulled his phone out of a pocket and looked at something on the screen. "We will meet him tonight at midnight."

I nodded and pulled out my own phone. "That will give us time to talk to her friends."

The pizza arrived when I was halfway down the short list and so far, no one had answered. I'd left a message to return my call and moved on each time. I didn't trust my judgment enough to leave any details. It occurred to me as I dialed the first number that Rio might have been taken by someone she thought of as a friend.

"Eat," Radim said, placing a slice on my plate.

I couldn't ignore the aroma: tomatoes, oil, and cheese.

Arugula was piled high on the crust and a drizzle of balsamic syrup. The crust was thin and had bubbles of air in the dough. I would never think of pizza at home the same way.

After downing the slice, I made the last calls. Only one answer and the woman had never heard of Rio. I hoped it didn't mean she'd been having an affair with a married man. I double checked the number and made a note beside it.

"We'll have to wait," I said. "That's becoming a regular state."

"Are your cases usually all action?" Radim asked.

"No," I said, taking another slice of the pizza. "It's not a TV show. But my cases don't usually involve a young girl's life in danger, and they aren't generally in a foreign country."

"Did your grandmother tell you about here?"

"Not much," I said. "She didn't like to talk about it. All I know is she escaped the regime, but I'm not clear which one."

"There have been many," he said. "Why are you here? I understand you are on vacation, but why Prague and not Barcelona, or the beaches of Portugal, or something more exotic?"

"I have a plan," I said, then took a bite of pizza to give me time to think. Having food in my stomach had done two things: made it possible for me to concentrate better and given me the impression I was safe. The second was just a dangerous fantasy.

"This is in your way?" he asked.

I knew he meant the case. Rio's problem wasn't in my way. I'd still be able to find somewhere to hide when we finished. It would be easier with Jack's money and I'd feel better about leaving if Rio was safe.

"No. I still have time. I quit my job," I said. "The plan was to come here and look for a place to buy. Something big that I could turn into an investment. Live a kinder life than I've been living."

He pushed the last of the pizza toward me. "I don't think you will enjoy peace and quiet for long."

"It would be fun to try," I said. "I thought I could rent out to people running retreats and conferences. Prague is fairly central. If I don't find something near here, I can still check out places in France and Italy."

"Then you promise me that you will join me for dinner in a year to prove you are not going mad with all the peace and quiet."

I laughed at that. Radim ordered coffee and I felt myself relaxing even more. A voice in the back of my head told me to be careful, but another said maybe if we knew more about each other, we might work together better. "The job was getting to the point where I felt dirty with every case."

"You were afraid to cross that line?"

I wouldn't tell him about what I did. The fewer people who learned, the safer I was. "It's possible I'm afraid of that switch you talked about."

"I remember that feeling," he said. "You know our history?"

"A bit, Nazis, communists, secret police."

"Yes. It is one thing to hear the facts, it is another to survive. I came close to turning that switch myself."

I didn't dig into his story for fear I'd end up telling mine.

Chapter 13

I spent the rest of the day in my room going through the contact names from Rio's book, and sleeping. I didn't get much off the names. A few were on Facebook and Instagram, but nothing posted with Rio or liked by her. The profile settings weren't public, so I couldn't do much stalking. I held out hope someone would call back tomorrow. If the numbers were some kind of code, I couldn't work it out. They weren't coordinates. They could be passwords, but with no indication of what they unlocked, they were useless.

Now it was almost midnight and I was waiting for Radim to meet me outside my hotel. There was something good about being able to walk everywhere, or at least everywhere so far. Vancouver was spread out and Prague seemed condensed. I missed the trees and the residential neighborhoods, but I could get used to tight and close buildings.

My mind was much clearer now, although I'm not sure my sleep patterns were being helped by restarting my day at almost midnight. It was out of my control, so I decided to worry about it when Rio was safe.

I figured we had enough to give Jack an update without going into names and hopes for success. I was texting a report to Jack when Radim walked up.

"You are ready?" Radim asked.

He didn't mean ready to go; he meant, had I made myself ready to let him lead the meeting tonight. "Are most of your contacts men?" I asked to avoid admitting I was not prepared to cede control.

"Some. Not all."

We crossed the street the locals called *The Ditch* and headed toward New Town.

"Why? Don't women have the skills you need?"

"Men are not as good at keeping their secrets," he said. "It's easier to make a deal with a man who has confessed his sins over too many beers."

"So, these contacts all come through blackmail?" I had a few like that. I didn't trust them as much. If I had leverage, someone else might have more. But most of my contacts were just trying to help or make amends.

"Mutual protection," he said. "Some grew up with me. We know our sins and try to keep them away from the light. Not everyone believes the past should be forgotten. Some of the new ones are the children of old friends. Some of them..."

"What?" I asked.

"Some of them found me because they needed a favor."

He led me around another corner, and I realized I'd never been in this part of the city. We passed The Globe bookstore a ways back. If we got separated, I would be in trouble. The only way I would be able to orient myself would be to go downhill and eventually arrive at the river.

"What about Maura?"

"Why are you so curious?" he asked.

"I'm not exhausted, so I can think straight. And I want to know who I'm dealing with."

He pointed to a building across the street. It was new and modern. Muscled men lurked in the doorway, like bouncers. No cars parked outside.

"Maura is a friend," he said. "If you want her story, ask her. Now you must be careful not to let your curiosity rule you. Remember what I said about Laszlo. He is unstable and dangerous."

"Laszlo?" This was the first time Radim had given this contact a name.

"That's all you need," he said. "Maybe more than you need. Don't let him know I told you his name. He will introduce himself. Don't be surprised if he uses a different identity."

Laszlo held my hand in both of his in that weird handshake that feels inappropriate and welcoming and a power play all at once. He was probably somewhere in his forties. He was pudgy, but not fat, his hair was black, his eyes brown, and his suit a shiny gray that I think is called sharkskin.

Radim introduced me as his partner, none of that awkwardness of defining what kind of partner that seemed to be important back home. He gave my first name only and Laszlo told me I was as beautiful as a Czech princess. I didn't cringe. He was clearly used to doing and saying what he wanted without correction, and if I showed my reaction, it would give him satisfaction that I wasn't willing to give.

The two women who lounged on a sofa in the corner agreed with him about my royalty when asked. I'm not sure they had the courage to do otherwise.

I looked as far from a princess as anyone could get. Although perhaps Czech princesses were not the same as the Disney version. Maybe they walked around in jeans and tee-shirts and traded glass slippers for boots.

"Let me pour us a glass of wine," Laszlo said. "I have a bottle here that I've saved for a special guest."

Radim glanced sideways at me, reminding me not to be fooled. I didn't need the reminder. Even though most of the really hard people I encountered tended to the silent and scary, I knew Laszlo's Bond Villain exterior could be covering something evil.

"Thank you," I said.

He opened the bottle, poured us glasses and insisted we sit on his balcony to see the city in all its resplendence. He actually used that word.

"Now, you say you need my help," Laszlo said when we'd offered all the right things about his view. "Tell me, Sharka, what is this problem?"

That blew the plan of me keeping quiet while Radim handled the psycho. I glanced at Radim and he shrugged.

"A girl has been taken," I said. "I need to find her and get her home to her family."

"A terrible situation," Laszlo said. "Prague is getting dangerous. Is that not right, my friend?"

Radim held up his glass as if to toast. "There was a time when the only danger was to your wallet," he said.

Laszlo smiled in blessing. "And times when we had nothing in our wallets to fear losing."

"The girl's father is worried," I said. "No one has made a ransom request yet. We have pictures of her after a beating." I held up my phone, offering to show him.

He recoiled. "I do not need proof, princess. This is terrible. What do you think I can do to help?"

It was like dealing with one of the partners in the law

firm. Never offering anything unless they danced around the facts for a while first. Laszlo knew something, otherwise we wouldn't be here. But I could see a blankness in his eyes. He felt nothing for Rio. I would need to figure out a way to flatter him into helping, or give him something he valued.

Radim might know what would work, but he was keeping out of it. "Her father can pay," I said.

Laszlo waved his hand to encompass the view of the city. "I have enough money," he said.

"What do you want?" I saw Radim narrow his eyes at me. Was he telling me to slow down? Well if he wanted that, he should step in and help.

"There are few things I want," Laszlo said. "Can you give me power over my competitors? Can you make me the most powerful man in Prague?" He laughed. "No, because I already have those things."

"Radim?" I asked, forcing him into the conversation.

"You can have a favor of a powerful man," he said.

Was he referring to himself, or did he think Jack would back him up? I didn't think Jack had any influence outside of the Canadian legal system despite my earlier comment.

"You and I have many favors between us," Laszlo said. "I believe you are still in my debt, yes?"

Radim nodded. "I am. But I meant the girl's father."

"And what is his name? Perhaps we are acquaintances."

"I doubt it," I said. Playing along with Radim's lie would be fun. "He usually sends an employee to Europe to deal with problems."

"And you are one of these employees, princess?" Laszlo refilled his glass. He didn't seem to notice that neither Radim nor I had even sipped our wine.

"No. I don't work for him. I'm doing him a favor." I slipped my phone from my pocket again.

"You are going to call him?" Laszlo asked. "Excellent. Tonight, I will make two new friends."

I flipped through my texts until I found the most recent picture of Rio. "I couldn't say no to helping her." I passed the phone to Laszlo.

He looked before remembering his ploy of being too delicate to see such horrors. I expected a slimy remark, not the sudden stillness. He paled and glared at Radim. "You knew who this was?"

"I know of the girl," he said.

"You must leave this alone," Laszlo said. "The stakes are too high for you to succeed."

I grabbed my phone back. "You know her?"

"She is looking into things best left secret," Laszlo said. He gulped down his wine and refilled his glass.

His tough facade dropped way faster than I imagined. He was truly scared. It couldn't be Rio's condition. As bad as it was, he should have seen worse, maybe done worse. I checked the picture again. Did he recognize the location? Did something tell him who took her?

"You must go now," Laszlo said. "Stay out of this... thing. If you continue, I do not want to be involved." He walked to the edge of the balcony and leaned on the rail.

"You know who did this?" Radim asked. "Tell us, Laszlo. She's just a girl. And she's a foreigner. If she dies, it will not disappear. The Canadians will ask questions. The government will be forced to look into it."

The last statement brought Laszlo back to us. "And they will come to me first," he said. "You know that."

"It is not the same," Radim said. "They won't drag you away. You've done nothing in this. Or are you involved?"

"No." His answer came fast.

"Then why are you afraid?" I asked. He was hiding something. Maybe he wasn't involved in the kidnapping, but he had some connection.

"I am not afraid," he said. "I am cautious." His face denied his words.

"Then why cautious?" I pressed. Radim didn't try to stop me. "Why would it be a problem if someone investigated?"

"Radim is only partly correct," Laszlo said. He knocked on the window and held up the empty bottle. One of the women hurried out with a fresh one. "It is true there is no secret police to spirit me away. But I could still go to prison. Your Al Capone was caught for something not so criminal." He looked at me over his full glass as though I was supposed to understand everything.

"Al Capone was American. Tax fraud is criminal." I waited.

"Yes. I suppose. But it still applies. There are things I did that cannot be proven and then there are things that can. The prison will not care which gets me locked up. In prison, I may not survive."

"So, we keep you out of it," I said. "No one but your people know we're here. That should satisfy you."

He looked to Radim, who nodded. "No one knows."

"I could have you killed and be sure I'm safe," Laszlo said.

"Not so easy," Radim said. "People will look for me. They know that you and I worked together in the past. They will come looking."

Laszlo drank half the glass and then refilled it. I took the bottle out of his reach. If he was trying to get too drunk to talk, it wouldn't work.

"So, I kill you after someone sees you leave," Laszlo said. "No more problem."

"You aren't going to do that," I said. "If you don't help us, and we get to leave, I'll send texts to everyone I know."

Laszlo sighed. "You are very difficult, princess."

"What do you know about this?" I asked. "We'll keep your secret. If you help us, there's no reason not to."

"Perhaps not a princess, but a warrior," Laszlo said. "Then it is on your head. It will not be me coming to kill you if things go wrong. And I will be gone from here before you can do me harm."

Chapter 14

"I don't know who this girl is," Laszlo said.

His immediate reaction pointed that out as a lie. I kept quiet, not wanting to interrupt the flow of his words.

He paced the balcony for a moment, then turned to face me. "Perhaps I am wrong. She is a student, yes?" He recovered fast. Probably the reason he thrived in his world.

Radim sat relaxed in his chair and watched Laszlo. Nothing about him showed urgency. It must be the right tactic for him, but I wasn't willing to let Laszlo waste our time. And my tactic wouldn't work if he calmed down.

"Yes. How did you know it was her?" I asked. I wished I'd thought to turn on the recording app earlier.

"You see on her shoulder." He pointed at my phone as though Rio's picture was showing. "That tattoo. That is how I know."

The small tattoo of a dove on Rio's shoulder had been there when I met her. "What about it?"

"It is how we were to look for her," he said. "We were ordered to find this girl and hold her. She discovered something that very dangerous people want to keep private."

"What did she discover? We don't have a lot of time here."

"This has to do with money," Laszlo said. "What do you know about how we move our finances?"

"Our? As in criminals? Big time criminals? Terrorists?"

"Did you think I was just a bystander?" Laszlo looked at Radim and shook his head. "You don't care enough about your princess to warn her about me?"

"I did. She is stubborn. Who wanted this girl?"

"The people who hide our money so the authorities can't trace it recently consolidated. Before, there were many players. We, the true criminals, not the terrorists, each had someone who would take care of laundering and paying." He poured more wine. His left eye drooped a little and his speech slowed. "Then a new agent came to us. His people offered a better return. We are the same as any businessmen; we pay as little as possible for the most benefit."

"So, you all moved your... business?" I hadn't expected this to be so mundane. "Now another player wants to take over, right? That's what she found."

"No, there is no new player. There can be no new player. This girl is the problem. She learned how they were doing it. She was clumsy and left traces."

"So, you do know her," I said.

Laszlo leaned in close to me. "No. I was made aware of her. I don't know her name or who she is."

Radim pressed his lips together and shook his head once. I couldn't react because Laszlo still stared at me, but I had more sense than to give him Rio's name.

"Did she threaten anyone with exposure?" The information still didn't make complete sense to me. "Did she try to take some of the money?"

Laszlo shrugged. "That I do not know. I suspect she is a threat even if it is simply in the minds of my colleagues."

"They are worried she'll do something," I said. I didn't know her well enough to say if the mysterious *they* were justified in their fear.

"Or perhaps those who currently provide the service are afraid of competition. I am aware how difficult the role would be to take over now. But is it not a truth that people in power most fear others with power?" Laszlo looked out over the city. "You do not need an education in finance these days. This girl has shown she holds the skills to set up as a competitor. Or, perhaps sell her knowledge to one."

Radim leaned forward, taking the wine and pouring the last into his glass. Laszlo made to summon another, but Radim stopped him. "You will be too drunk to run."

"If there is competition now, it will be chaos. Consolidating to one agent went smoothly. None of the launderers we used before were powerful enough to win a fight to keep their business. They moved on to other interests or joined the new organization."

"This time there is enough power," Radim said. "Chaos is when people die. Criminals are like anyone; they want stability. They will fight change."

"Yes," Laszlo said. "I think it is time for me to move my operations out of the city until this is over."

"If they want to find you, it will not be difficult." Radim tilted his head toward the room. "How cheaply do you think your friends in there will sell you out?"

"Not as quickly as I can dispose of them," Laszlo said. "Are we finished?"

The way he casually threatened to kill his employees chilled me. He had used the same tone as if he was asking the time. Radim told me Laszlo was dangerous, and now I saw just how bad it would be if he wanted us gone. The man had no feeling for anyone. Talking to us had let him show off his power, and his ego fed on the attention. The fear he'd shown at Rio's picture was real, but not enough to tell us everything he knew, or anything useful in finding her.

Leaving was the safest option, but safety didn't matter. I still needed answers. Something to get us closer to saving Rio.

"If it's so risky, why did you agree to talk?" I didn't think it was the wine. Any good actor could fake drunkenness and someone in Laszlo's position would be a great actor if only to hide his fear. He seemed sober enough now. I hoped the scare made him careless.

"I want to survive the coming chaos." He stood and ushered us back into the living room.

"I would be surprised if you didn't," Radim said.

"Now I have warning. That gives me options."

The women on the couch stood as Laszlo entered. One of them moved our way, her eyes unfocused with drugs. The other lay back and watched.

"Why are you making us wait, lover?" the woman said. She reached to caress Laszlo's shoulder.

He pushed her away hard enough that she fell. She didn't object or cry out. She twisted on the floor like she was performing a yoga move and crawled back to the couch.

Radim put his hand on my arm and gave a tiny shake of his head. I didn't need the advice. She chose to be here. It didn't make the abuse right, but...

"That's right, princess. You want to save her, yes?" Laszlo didn't even look at the woman.

"She knows it is your business how you use your property," Radim said.

I let him take over. If I said anything, I'm not sure I

would be able to stop myself from punching the creep, no matter what I thought. And Laszlo was looking for a reason to deal with me. I was okay until he decided he could act without a reason.

"So, you go now," Laszlo said. "I think we are closer to even now, Radim. You owe me less than you did before."

Radim's hand tightened on my arm. "We can check the balance of favors when this is over. Perhaps tonight we saved your life. Is that worth anything to you?"

Laszlo laughed and slapped Radim on his shoulder. "My friend, you know it is. I can only hope my continued existence is still valuable to other people. As you say, we will make a reckoning when it is safe."

"Do you have any idea where they might be keeping the girl?" I asked "You have your warning, but we only have the answer to why she was taken. We can't save her unless we know who did it and where she is."

Laszlo walked us to the door. "You think I care about this girl? Not as much as I care about my life. I do not know who ordered her kidnapping. The instructions came from a middle man. No one knows who runs that organization. We only know who represents our interests. They only know who they pass the money on to."

"Like a terrorist cell?" I asked. My mouth was getting out of control, but Laszlo was talking, and provoking him seemed to be the key to keeping the words flowing.

Laszlo didn't take offense, or didn't show that he had. "Or a resistance group. This method was not invented by terrorists. Only at the end does it become clear who are the good guys and who the bad. The model worked well for centuries."

"What about the thugs who took her, not who ordered it?" I couldn't leave without at least one piece of information.

"Your hero would know this the same way I do," Laszlo said, flicking a glance at Radim.

"Yes, now we are sure why," Radim said. "There are people I can check with. People who are not so closely tied to the problem."

Laszlo gave us a huge sigh and slumped his shoulders: still acting. "I am not the problem, Radim. You and I both know how easy it is to become a criminal; sometimes just because the rules have changed, yes?"

"Where might they take her?" I asked. This mysterious past of bad decisions and mistakes was getting on my nerves. I didn't need to know their history, just what they could do to help. If Laszlo felt calm enough to put on his arch villain act again, we were running out of time.

"There are old buildings that no one enters," Laszlo said. "Radim will know more about it than I do now." He opened the door and practically pushed us through.

"How would they find out about the rooms?" Radim asked.

"Not everyone who used them turned respectable," Laszlo said, turning the last word into a slur. "They tell their kids when the time comes."

I turned to ask what he meant but he spoke first.

"I have no more answers for you," he said. "I am leaving the city. Go, before I decide you know too much for my safety."

Chapter 15

Radim and I stood on the street, which for a change was quiet. Maybe Laszlo kept people away to support his pretense that he lived in a peaceful neighborhood.

"What did he mean," I asked, "when he said you would know where they kept her?"

He urged me toward the main street. I couldn't remember the name, but I was getting better at orienting myself by landmarks, not addresses.

"Everyone did things to survive under the communists," he said. "Under the Nazis too, but I'm too young for those memories."

I could see he was making a poor attempt at humor. "No one is questioning what you did. I have things I prefer to leave buried too. But that's not helping us find Rio."

We were around crowds again. Not so thick as midday, but still a comfort until I realized most of them were drunk enough to fall down and the rest were only a drink or two away from it. Radim kept walking and I followed behind, once again feeling like I'd handed over control. He entered a park and found us a bench. The park wasn't filled with groups of shifty people like I'd expect in downtown Vancouver at one thirty in the morning. The lack of people didn't stop me from being nervous and keeping my eyes on the shadows.

"I think I might know of a place," Radim said. "When you asked about the men who took her, the ones with the van, I realized we were looking in the wrong place with Laszlo."

"We got something out of it. He gave you an idea. You think this might not be the people he's afraid of? That someone is acting on their own?"

"Laszlo thought that at the end," Radim said. "That's why he reminded me of the buildings."

If the kidnapping was about someone trying to steal from people as powerful as Laszlo said, this might all be about money. They might be stupid too; I tried not to think about how dangerous stupid criminals could be. I needed to believe Jack would pay and Rio would go on with her life.

"It answers a lot of questions," I said. "If they are rogue players, the whole delay in asking for the ransom would be about making sure they wouldn't be traced."

"But if they are crazy enough to steal from this organization, we can't be sure how far they will go."

"So, it's gotten more dangerous and more hopeful at the same time," I said.

"Yes."

"How certain are you about this place? That it's where they are holding Rio?"

"Laszlo said there are a few old buildings left where secrets can be kept." Radim rubbed his face and then looked at the ground. "And now we think this is not some grand conspiracy. Not everyone knows about these rooms, but I do, and it is possible the kidnappers do. The place I am thinking about is close to here. It would be a good place to hide someone, not pleasant but safe."

The way he avoided looking at me made me think he had done exactly that in the past.

I pulled out my phone. The professional in me said it was time to report to Jack. It was daytime in Vancouver, and he'd left us alone long enough to worry me. The respite wouldn't last long; he was too controlling to stay out of the action for much longer. Another part of me wanted to wait until we had more than an assumption that we'd found her. It felt cruel to raise his hopes only to destroy them later. I wanted Jack out of my life, but I didn't want to be spiteful.

"What will you tell him?" Radim asked.

"Jack?" How did he guess?

"Who else would you call?"

Michael, but I didn't say that. "I need to tell him we've made some progress." The professional side won. I learned early in my career that leaving the client in the dark was always the wrong thing to do. But I didn't need to speak to him.

We are making progress. Going silent for a while. I sent the text and turned the phone off.

"How far?" I asked. "Why can't we go now?"

Radim stood and cocked his head down the slope of the park. "Not far. I can't say if a better time will come. Unless you changed your mind and want the police to hear what is happening."

"Lead the way," I said, sounding more confident than I felt. "Are we headed for a secret entrance?"

He chuckled. "Yes, but not as I expect you imagine."

No matter what I tried, he wouldn't tell me more.

What did he think I imagined? This city didn't have large residential areas where a front yard gets overgrown, giving criminals places to lurk. Most buildings emptied onto the sidewalk. In fact, I couldn't see how anything secret could happen around here; too many windows, too many people.

We headed back toward the river again. This time I decided to work on my navigation skills. According to my phone, we were heading south and west. I tried to identify the streets but gave up when I realized they all had names, not numbers. Mispronouncing names wouldn't help me find Radim if we got separated.

He turned a few corners and I had to reorient myself. I missed the mountains as a tool to negotiate my way. I gave up on the phone." Where are we going?"

"You know the city?"

"Yeah, enough. Old Town, New Town, Lesser Town." It didn't seem as vague when the words formed in my head. "Fine. I don't. But if you aren't with me, I can't risk getting lost."

"This is a part of Prague the tourists don't visit much, no sights to photograph, no stories for the guides to invent. Lots of buildings are left as they stood decades ago. Some old people live here, but mostly it's empty apartments and churches."

"So, this building is which one of those?" He hadn't given me any information, so my brain had conjured up a house.

"An apartment building."

He walked a little faster. I figured it was so I couldn't keep asking questions. I went back to trying to read street signs. I could tell we were in the new part, but new is relative, I guess. Most of the buildings looked hundreds of years old.

It was an apartment building, but I'm not sure it was

ever a desirable place to live. There were tenants; some of
the windows showed light, and I heard pop music coming
from above us. The lobby wallpaper peeled from damp,
and the floor was covered with tiles that had not been
cleaned in a long time. Maybe they'd been yellow when
new, but now they showed a grimy gray, although that
might be the lighting. A couple of fixtures came on when
we entered, but they flickered, and more were broken than
working.

"Who lives here?"

"Refugees or migrant workers." Radim crossed the
lobby and unlocked a door in the corner across from the
stairs. "When I used it, we would pay the caretaker to let us
through."

Behind the door was a set of concrete steps. I heard a
click and then a buzz. Radim had turned on the light. Two
bare bulbs hanging on an exposed wire. The music cut off
as the door closed behind us.

I was not willing to just go down into the basement. "Is
this storage?"

"No one comes here," he said.

"So, who keeps the lights on?"

"Lights work for a long time if they are not turned on."

"And you think the kidnappers came here? How did
they learn this place existed?"

Radim touched my elbow and it brought me back to
the reality that I was not in a horror movie. No matter
what was down in the dark, it was human. "Go down,
please."

I moved quickly, wanting to get this over with. I
planned to keep him talking; silence just made my fears
grow. "And how would they learn of it?"

"I was one of four people who knew about this place.
Some of them had kids."

"Was Laszlo one of the four?"

"No."

At the bottom, another string of bulbs lit up a corridor lined with rotting wooden storage shelves on one side and a door at the end. I wished I had a gun. Not that I wanted to kill anything, but having a weapon might put an end to the creepy story running in my head.

"The room is soundproof," he said. "Only one way in and the lock is strong."

"You have this key too?"

"Why would I bring you here if I didn't?"

He stepped past me and slid a key in and opened the door. I guess getting upgrades on the security of a secret room was impossible.

Inside, the room was unfinished. Stone walls and floor made me think the apartment had been built on top of a dungeon. Maybe it had. The lights came on. More bare bulb and wire decorating.

A chair sat in the middle of the room. Splotches of brownish red that could only have been blood splattered around the floor. The smell was coppery and sour.

"We missed her," I said.

"We missed someone. You think this kidnapping is the only crime committed in the city?"

Good point.

Radim walked over to the chair. He touched the stain underneath and muttered something. Then he picked up a small square from the seat, being careful not to make much contact with the surface.

"The blood is dry," he said. "The new blood. No one cleans up after they are done in here." He handed me the square.

It was an SD card; clean despite the blood. Rio didn't drop this as a clue. It had been left here on purpose for us to find. We didn't have any way of reading the SD card in here, but I needed some proof.

I couldn't work on just the assumption that the blood was Rio's. There wasn't enough of it to make me fear she'd been killed.

"Anything else? Anything that would prove she was here, and that this isn't some random horror pit?"

He was searching the floor closer than I would have liked to get. I paced around the walls of the room. The bulb was too weak to help much. I saw nothing but a few bits of stone and balls of fabric. I looked over to Radim, who was inspecting the underside of the seat. "We need more light."

"I have found nothing more," he said, placing the chair back on its legs.

I pulled out my phone and turned on the flashlight app. It would use up more battery than I liked, but I had no choice.

I shone the beam into the corners and then along the wall. A tiny circle of dark metal caught my attention. I flipped through my texts as I bent to pick it up. "She was here," I said, checking the first picture of Rio. "This was in her lip. Someone warned them we were coming. Why else would they leave?"

"It seems so."

"You said Laszlo didn't use this room. Did he know the location?" The number of people in the loop on the investigation was small enough to make me worry about each one of them.

He shoved his hands in his jacket pocket. "He's the one who sent us here, but everyone knows the rooms still exist, just not where."

"Would he warn them?"

Radim shrugged. "It doesn't make sense. He pointed us here. Why?"

"Maybe they were supposed to kill us?"

"He could have done that in his apartment. The bodyguards are experts in cleaning up his messes."

Chapter 16

"We will find nothing else here," Radim said. "Let's go to my apartment. We can read the card in my computer."

I didn't want to stay here any longer than I had to. I'm not superstitious normally, but I felt like the echoes of all the screams from all the people who were tortured in this room rang in my head. The place had no other purpose, no storage, no hide and seek refuge. I wondered if Radim had been in the chair or doing the torturing, or both.

He lived in a nicer area. Uphill from where we started, and toward the National Museum. A clean building with a working elevator, no odor, and clean floors. Inside was small. A living room, bathroom, tiny kitchen, and a bedroom. Not that different from Rio's place, except no one had ransacked it. He had a few pictures on the wall, mostly sites around the city. But there was one of him with a group of friends. Interesting that the faces of the others had been blurred enough so I couldn't see the features. I guess he knew who they were.

He powered up his laptop while I washed my hands in an effort to shed the slimy feeling of the room where Rio was beaten. When I got to the living room, Radim had two mugs of tea on the table along with his computer.

"I don't drink tea."

"Ginger tea," he said. "Good for you." He held out his hand for the SD card.

I passed it to him and took a mug. This was nothing like tea as I remembered it. Little chunks of ginger soaked in hot water, and some lemon by the aroma of the steam. I took a sip. "Delicious," I said. That didn't really describe the reaction I had. It was like the tea cleaned the stench of violence from my soul.

Radim clicked on the only file on the card. The screen filled with Rio's battered face: a video. "Ready?" he asked, finger hovering over the play button.

"No. But go ahead."

Rio cried in big gulping sobs. Her hands tied behind her back, she slumped on the chair. "Please, help me," she managed to squeeze out the words through swollen lips.

A hand flashed into the scene, catching her with a back-handed slap.

"They want money," she said. "Please, tell my father. He'll pay."

They must have figured out that Jack had someone here looking for his daughter. It explains why they left a card and didn't send a video directly to Jack. They were taking a big risk expecting it to be retrieved. If we hadn't found the place, they wouldn't have this leverage.

Another figure moved into sight. A man, but he was dressed in black with a black ski mask and black gloves. He grabbed her wrists and pulled them up. Rio screamed. He said something quietly to her.

"He says not to interfere," Rio translated in a broken voice. "They will tell Dad how much and where to deliver it. If you don't follow orders, they will kill me."

She started sobbing again and no matter what the man did, he couldn't force her to tell us more. The video ended.

"That was the room," I said. "I mean, they didn't film in her new location, right? They did it there."

"Long enough ago that the blood dried," Radim said. "The ring was in her lip when they filmed."

"You think she found a way to remove it and leave it as a clue?" I didn't think you could do that with your hands behind your back, but she might have bitten the ring open and spat it into the corner. Most likely it came off during the beating.

"I need to watch it again." He looked at me and I realized he thought I couldn't take it.

"Okay," I said. While he watched, I listened and looked up how long blood took to dry.

"The man spoke Czech," Radim said.

"They left at least two hours ago according to this wiki entry," I said. "What did he say to her?"

"Just what she told us. I was hoping to recognize the voice."

"No luck?"

"He was young, in his early twenties at most."

"That is a problem," I said. An older guy would have more life experience, understand how far to go and when to stop — and maybe wouldn't be impulsive. The fact that he was young and taking this kind of risk meant he could be unstable. "Drugs?" I asked. If he was high, Rio's situation was only going to go from bad to horrifying.

"I don't think so. He was calm." Radim copied the video to his computer. "Maybe she will be okay if they think the money is coming."

I didn't want to believe that Jack would let his daughter die if the ransom was too much; his silence did nothing to alleviate my fears.

"You should send him this," Radim said. "The video was meant for him. To give the message. To make him pay."

"Watching might just make things worse with him," I said. "He hasn't responded to my last text."

"It doesn't matter." Radim copied the video into a file sharing account. "Send him the link. Tell him to get a lot of money ready. See what he says."

And what if he doesn't respond? That kind of thinking didn't help. I had to believe Jack wasn't lying about Rio being more important than any amount of cash.

"Not yet," I said. "Let me check with Michael. I need to find out what's going on with Jack first." And I needed to be sure that he wasn't on a plane and coming here. That would explain his lack of response.

I sent the text before I checked the local time. Just after work, so anyone I contacted should be available. Whether they would respond was another thing.

"What about Rio's mother?"

"Died," I said. "When Rio was five. In a car accident."

"No other relatives?"

"As far as I can tell, Rio is the latest in a long line of only children. Jack's parents passed a few years ago: dad from cancer, mother from heart problems."

"Being alone in the world must be hard," Radim said.

"What about you?" I assumed he was alone like me, but I didn't want to talk about me. "Family?"

"A few cousins in Germany. Mostly, I have friends."

"Me too," I said, because it seemed rude not to.

"So, do you know anyone who would do this?" I needed to sleep but couldn't risk missing a call. Talking helped. "The kidnapping? On someone's orders? Just to grab a lot of money?"

"I know people who know people." He pulled out his

phone. "But, people like this? I haven't a clue who to contact to even ask about them."

"Can you tell if the guy who spoke on the video is from around Prague?" The words all sounded the same to me, but I assume English was the same to people who didn't speak it. They probably wouldn't be able to tell an east coast accent from a west coast one.

He played the video again, looking away from the scene to listen closer. "No. He has a little accent, but not enough. I think they are Czech, the way he speaks is... *hovorový*. I don't know the word in English. Local to here is the best."

"Colloquial. He uses words and expressions only used in the city?"

"Yes. I would be happier if he was not Czech," Radim said.

Michael called before I could suggest we review the video again. I felt like a coward for being relieved.

"Jack is acting nervous," Michael said. "But not so much that if I didn't know about Rio, I wouldn't think it out of the ordinary. He's usually a bit tightly wound before court."

"He hasn't called or returned my texts. Any idea why?" There was a chance Jack was in court.

"He's been in his office all day. The door locked. I've seen him maybe twice, and only on the way to the toilet."

I told him what we'd found. "I don't want to send the file to Jack and find out it disappeared into the silence."

"Forward it to me."

Radim forwarded Michael the file before I could say yes or no.

"I'll give it to Jack, and I'll find out what's going on," Michael said. "How bad is she?"

"Bad," Radim said. "Almost as bad as Elijah."

"I'll prepare him," Michael said. "You think she's still alive?"

"Yes," I said. "But Jack isn't aware that you're helping. I can tell him if he calls me."

"Not to worry," Michael said. "I'll tell him that you reached out when he decided to ignore you. A bit of guilt is a good motivator."

"I wish I could be in the office to see his reaction." *Or give him a kick in the ass.*

"I don't care how he takes the news. I'm pretty much done with this firm too," Michael said. "I found a few other opportunities that sound more interesting. When we're finished with this, I'm gone."

"Hey, you won't disappear on me, right?" I had no idea he was planning to go. Of course, he had no idea I was going either.

"Did you plan to keep in touch with me, or anyone here?"

"With you, yes," I said. "I want to be part of your network of friends." As I said the words, I realized the truth. There were a few people who I didn't want to cut off from my life.

"Okay, good to know I'm not just anybody," Michael said.

"What about the texts? The ones from before?" Radim asked. "Did you find out where they came from? Or who sent them?"

"Still trying. Any news on your end?"

"Not yet," Radim said.

"Do I know who you asked?"

If Michael knew Radim's contacts, why had he kept that back? I stopped asking myself questions I didn't know the answers to. They only fed my paranoia.

"I stick to my rules." He grinned. "I'll tell him you've found nothing."

I noticed how they hid the names of the mysterious friends. Would I become one of them? Would I be asked to hide someone or something? I had no skills in hacking, and I wouldn't believe Michael or Radim were the kind of people to assassinate someone, so I had limited value.

"If I'm going to catch Jack before he leaves, I need to go," Michael said. "I'll text you with an update on how it goes."

"Where would they have moved her?" I asked. The sun was starting to chase the darkness away and now the investigation was on its third day. This was when the ransom demand should come in. This could be the last few hours we would have to find Rio before the drop. Maybe her last few hours of life.

"There are more places like that building," Radim said. "I don't have any information on them. I don't know anyone who knew of more than one."

"Like the money launderers. You were separated into cells, and you only met the people in yours."

"Yes, but it's not that simple." Radim pulled a sheet of paper from under his laptop. He drew three circles on it, not touching and not too far apart. "This is what you described, yes?"

I agreed with him and saw what he meant. "Someone has to be talking to the other cells. Like Laszlo explained, someone coordinates between the customer and the business." Taking it down to a commercial example helped clear my mind of the 'product' these people handled.

"Exactly. So, in one cell, you have at least four people." He put smaller circles inside each one. "Now if you are a member of one cell, you are sure someone is this liaison. But you can be certain only that it is you or not."

"So, you can't take over the cell, but you can still inform on the other members," I said.

"There is also someone who is spying on your cell. The Communists taught us that if you are not spying for someone, they are spying on you."

"That's why you have four minimum, not three," I said. "If you aren't the liaison, you know one of the others is, and if you are not spying for someone, you can be sure someone else is." It was starting to become too convoluted for me to imagine the whole thing working.

"When you apply it to criminals, it is less complicated. In communism, everyone was spying, so you didn't trust anyone. Not even family. If you got caught doing anything wrong, you disappeared, or you died."

"Criminals are different," I said. "If you get caught by the cops, you can make a deal and disappear in the right way. If you get caught by the boss, you're likely to be killed."

"Yes. There is another difference. Everyone was involved when we were under Russia's thumb. Only criminals are involved in this."

I drank the last of the ginger tea; even cold it was refreshing. "That means some of them are intelligent and some are not. And the ones who aren't tend to act on impulse."

He tapped the paper. "Maybe that is what happened? A couple of lower level criminals decided that they need to take some control."

"Things aren't getting more optimistic for Rio," I said. "Jack should have called by now."

"Michael will make him. It's possible that Jack is out, yes?"

"Yes." He should be sitting by the phone waiting for

someone to contact him. I guess he could be doing that anywhere. "I need some air."

"I think I can make some calls," Radim said. "I might be able to find one of the liaisons from the old days. It might lead us to another room. But if you need to go out, it can wait."

"I'll be fine on my own." I needed to test my landmarks. And I wanted to see if Laszlo was gone yet. Radim wouldn't let me go if he knew.

I only made two wrong turns finding my way back to Laszlo's apartment. Wrong turns that taught me something, so not completely a waste.

I suspected what was going on when I was a few blocks away.

Smoke in the air.

Two fire trucks waited on the road outside. A small crowd of spectators gathered as close as the firemen allowed. Ashy water ran down the face of the building and into a drain half a block away.

The firemen were wrapping up, one of them talking to a couple of cops. I slipped into the group watching.

"What happened?" I asked in my most innocent voice.

A man carrying a tiny dog in his arms turned to me. "An hour ago. It was bad."

"Was anyone hurt?" I was so grateful he spoke English I wanted to hug him.

"The police just arrived."

I was grateful that English was common, as the others offered their own theories and I could understand them. Arson, gang fighting, gas leak, faulty electrical. Funny how tragedy encouraged people to talk.

The cops and firemen were arguing but we stood too far away for my buddy to make out the words.

Then two ambulance attendants carried a body bag on

a stretcher out of the building and I realized they were fighting about safety and evidence. The cops wanted to keep the body in place for the investigation, the firemen wouldn't let anyone who wasn't critical into the area until it was safe. I'd heard the same thing before in an arson case Jack defended.

In the next ten minutes, four more body bags went into ambulances that drove away without their sirens or lights. Three women from the couch, two bodyguards. Laszlo made sure he got away clean.

I drifted out of the crowd and headed back to Radim's.

Chapter 17

When I got back, Radim stood at the window making calls, trying to find a lead, a name, a next step. He spoke in Czech, so I was left with nothing to do and I needed to hide my lingering reaction to the fire.

I took his laptop and started researching money laundering, recent arrests, any clue leading to the names of the players. I didn't find much. I discovered I still had access to some police databases by signing in. Money laundering was a federal crime, so the information covered the world, or at least the part of the world that reported. Searching for a lead on the bosses would be futile. Like most criminal activity, the low-level people get arrested and the cops want to use them to get the people running the organization. So, any names that might help had been changed, codes used to keep them anonymous. If I had days, or weeks, I could persuade someone to give me a name, but we didn't have that long.

Jack's firm had defended a few of the cases in Canada. They were a high-profile firm, so I wasn't surprised. I could ask Jack about the clients, but I didn't hold onto much hope Jack knew of a connection between Vancouver and Prague. My best guess was the people in charge were located in Europe and Asia; the money was there, and it's got to be easier to conceal illegal gains in large transactions.

"If Michael can give us a location on the texts, will that help you figure it out?" I asked when Radim ended his most recent call.

"Perhaps. He seems to have contacts in many places."

"More like a network of hackers and spies," I said. "I guess we're lucky he's more the superhero than the super villain type."

"When I first met him, he faced that choice," Radim said. "Someone in his past must have taught him the difference between right and wrong. Life can be as simple as choosing to wait for justice instead of taking revenge."

I faced that same choice two weeks ago; Laszlo faced it last night. "Sometimes life gives you chances to retreat from a bad decision."

"Not many," he said as though he knew exactly what I meant.

This case was my chance at redemption. "Did you find out anything from your calls?"

"No one knows anything," he said. "It doesn't mean someone won't call with information later."

"It will be over today," I said. "I don't think we'll be looking for her tomorrow."

He turned away from the window and saw my expression. "What happened?"

How was I so transparent? I considered lying for a moment but realized he would catch me. "I went back to Laszlo's."

"I told you this was dangerous. You need to trust me, Sharka. What did he do?"

My throat tightened with emotion. I took a deep breath to stop myself from choking on the words. "He burned the place down with people inside."

He didn't yell or seem surprised. He nodded thoughtfully and sat beside me. "You should not have gone back."

"Yes. I heard your warning. I'm not even sure I would have gone inside if he was there."

"You would be dead if you had. Not then, but Laszlo would have had someone watching. He would stop anyone who might lead the police to him."

"Would they have seen me in the crowd?"

"Watching is okay. It sends a message."

The fact he didn't fight made me furious. It wasn't fair or reasonable, but I was tired and frustrated and afraid. "Don't you think I know I'm an idiot?" Lashing out was supposed to make me feel better, but it didn't.

"Will you trust me next time? Or am I going to need to keep two women safe?"

I stood up so fast I felt the chair rock behind me. "I don't need you to keep me safe. I am fully competent to take care of myself."

He held up his hands. "I agree. You need to start doing it."

I deflated. A good fight needed two people and he chose not to play. "Fine."

"What will you do when this is over?" he asked. "Will you finish your holiday and go home?"

Before I got out an answer, he went to the kitchen. I followed. Maybe the lack of sleep made me feel this way, or the fact we'd been together for so many hours and seen such awful things, I felt like we were friends. Not close ones, but definitely not just two people doing a job. And the sudden change of subject woke up my rational side. I was hungry and my temper always won over my sense when I needed food.

"You like eggs?" Radim asked as he pulled a pan out of a cupboard.

"Breakfast would be great," I said. "Let me help."

"You set the table, I cook," he said. He told me where to find plates and cutlery, dropped bread into a toaster that looked antique, and grabbed a container of eggs from the fridge.

Within ten minutes we were seated with plates of eggs and sausage in front of us, a stack of toast on a plate in the middle. Coffee, butter and marmalade all ready to be eaten, more calories than I would normally eat in a day. I figured it might be a long time before I ate again, so I was grateful for the feast.

"Yes," I said as I buttered a slice of toast. My plan to just run away needed changing. I had to close off some open threats before I disappeared. "You asked if I would go back to Vancouver after this is over."

"You will finish your holiday?"

Would I be able to settle back into vacation mode when Rio's case was done? "There are a few things I'd like to do before I go back."

"Like what? The city has attractions, but there are other places to see." He took our coffee cups into the kitchen to refill.

I liked this. Chatting over breakfast. I felt comfortable. I couldn't forget Rio's plight, but it didn't consume me. That would change as soon as either of our phones pinged.

"I'm only going back to Vancouver to make sure I can leave without regret," I said. "I'm ready for a new life. I'm going to look for a place to buy."

"What was your grandmother's name?" he asked. "You

think you still have some relatives here? I could find them for you."

"I'm pretty sure she was the only one who survived." She'd told me about the way people had disappeared.

"I could still ask my contacts. Maybe I could also help you find a new home. What part of the city?"

The comfortable feeling was wearing thin. We were getting close to things I didn't want to talk about. "Not the city," I said. "I want a big house in the country, remember? To relax, peace and quiet and all that."

"You think you are ready for such a life? It is a huge change from investigation. You won't get bored?"

I thought about the fee Jack agreed to pay. "I can always move on if I do."

"Okay. Some of my friends are in the country. I can help with that too." He picked up the empty plates.

"You cooked, I wash up," I said.

I STOOD AT THE WINDOW, looking down into the street. A few people walked past, all dressed for work. Most of the traffic was delivery trucks. The tourists were all tucked into bed or eating their buffet breakfasts. Rain started to fall, and I wondered if the streets would be less crowded because of it.

I guess all cities have this same moment, when it feels like the day is fresh and everything is a new start. My phone was charging on the table. I checked the battery. Full charge.

Michael called.

"You found something?" I asked. Radim looked up from his research.

"A location," he said, "and something odd."

I put the call on speaker. "Radim is here."

"We managed to find a location for the phones sending the texts." Michael texted me a photo of a map with an area circled. "We can't get any closer than that."

I expanded the picture and saw the circle enclosed about four blocks square. Or what would be, if the city was set up in a grid. "This is better than what we had before."

"I gave Jack the update," Michael added.

Jack hadn't called me. "How long ago?"

"A little over an hour. I don't think he was surprised."

"You're saying he might already have that video?" I asked. "And he didn't contact me?"

"That's the weird thing. He sent a text to the number I started tracing a couple of minutes after I left his office."

"He would have just replied to a text, correct?" Radim asked. "It does not mean he knew who he was calling."

"Yes, but is it what you'd expect from the father of a teenage girl who'd been battered and terrified? When he had competent people nearby?"

Nothing Jack had done since he'd called me two days ago made sense. "Is there any chance you can see what he sent?"

"Not without taking his phone. And my pickpocketing skills are rusty."

"Do you think he's undermining us? It is possible he has someone else working on it." If Jack didn't trust me to do the job, he would only screw things up.

"All I can do is guess, Sharka. Yes, he's acting odd, but no more so than Jack usually acts."

I looked at Radim, but he had nothing to offer. "There's something going on, Michael. If I ignore my suspicion, it might mean Rio dies."

"How do you suggest I find out?" Michael asked. "If he owns another burner phone, I can't find a record. I could look through his accounts to see if he's paid someone a chunk of money."

"We still couldn't be sure it was about Rio," Radim said.

They were right. Talking about it just wasted time, but until we had a lead, there was nothing else for us to do. "Just keep watching him." I chose to hang onto my suspicions for a while longer.

"Do you know the neighborhood?" I asked Radim.

"A little," he said. "I don't know of any safe house in the area, but we can figure it out, yes? They wouldn't be able to take Rio into a hotel. That will narrow things a little.

My phone buzzed: Jack.

"He's finally made contact, Michael. I'll call you later if there's anything we need."

"Be careful," Michael said, then disconnected.

Chapter 18

"Jack," I said. He hadn't earned a polite greeting. "You saw the video."

"You shouldn't have brought Michael into this. Every time you bring someone in, there's a bigger risk that the police will find out."

"Michael can be trusted," I said. "I can't do this alone. Did *you* bring anyone else in?"

"No. I'm thinking about doing so; I need results."

"If I'm going to do this job, I need to know everything that's happening. If you've got another investigator working on the case, they'll be in my way."

"Competition makes you work faster," Jack said.

"No. Adding another investigator complicates things and increases the risk. If you sent someone else here, we should work together."

"Fine. You are the only one so far."

I didn't know if I could believe him. If it was the truth, there was still no guarantee he wouldn't. All I could hope for was that he would remember what I said. As much as I tried, I couldn't hold out much hope.

"Just answer my texts so I know what's going on."

"I'm paying you. Did you forget? I call the shots."

"I'm trying to save your daughter."

"Why am I on speaker?"

"I need my hands free to make notes." I was not going to get into a tangent of explaining Radim.

"I got a call."

Why didn't he start with that? "What do they want?"

"They've figured out someone is looking for Rio. They want to meet you. They want something delivered."

"Okay, is this the ransom?"

"They don't want money," Jack said. "They want to see you."

To see me?

"Is that what they said, exactly?"

I wondered if what they wanted was to kill me. As soon as the thought crossed my mind, I knew I was wrong. If they killed me, no one would be able to deliver the ransom and they'd want it paid in cash, because every electronic transaction is eventually traceable. People hid money hoping the cops would give up following false leads. My RCMP contacts hinted that strategy worked until the value reached more than a hundred million. Then it becomes worth the cost to investigate.

"Yes. Word for word."

I looked at Radim to see if I was the only one sensing the lie. He was busy searching maps of the area Michael had identified for us.

"Did they send a text?"

"No. I received a phone call."

"Did you record it?" The company desk and mobile phones had been set to record calls automatically. You could delete the recording afterward, but surely Jack couldn't be that stupid.

"I own a private phone. They called me on that."

"How did they get the number?" I needed to tell Michael about this.

"Probably from Rio. She is probably telling them everything she knows. Stop asking questions."

"I need that number, Jack."

"No."

"Did you contact them?" I had to know if he'd tell me the truth.

There was a long pause. "No," he said.

If I called him on the lie, it would expose Michael's full involvement and end up in another argument. "What did you say when they contacted you?"

"It doesn't matter," he said. "You simply need to meet them and hand over Rio's passwords."

"Jack, everything matters. You want Rio back, so you need to keep me informed." I'd said the words so many times since this started that I heard defeat in my voice, like I said it with no confidence he would toe the line.

"You think I don't want her back?" This time he was shouting. My hope of avoiding a battle died. "This is bigger than just her kidnapping. I want Rio back and I need things done so she'll be safe. You let me decide what information you need."

I hated being shouted at. I wanted to yell back and tell him to shove his problem. I wanted to hang up and let him figure out how else to save his daughter. But I knew that wasn't rational. Even if he was an expert at pushing my buttons, I couldn't let Rio become collateral damage of my reaction. I had to control my temper. Jack was an asshole and he only got worse under stress. Or maybe I no longer cared to put up with it.

"Where do they want to meet?"

"You have her codes?"

"Yes, where do they want to meet?" I would ask as many times as he made me.

"The old Jewish cemetery," he said. "They want you to go alone. They want you to bring her access codes. All of them."

"Will she be there?" If we had an opportunity to take her back, we could be done.

"They said no." Jack sighed; the anger burned out of his words.

"Okay. When?"

"They said, 8 AM your time."

"We need proof that she's still alive." The words were hard to say, but Jack had seen the video; he couldn't ignore the chance Rio was dead.

"Don't risk her life by arguing with them." The heat had returned. "You just take her codes and meet them. You do everything they say."

It was after six now. That didn't leave much time to set something up to make sure I was safe. "How will you know it's done?"

"They said they would contact me." He took a breath. "Just do what they ask. I want her back."

I didn't have a choice. He was holding something back. Spending time trying to force him to tell me what it was only put Rio at more risk. I'd been worrying that we had nothing to follow up and now we did. We could trail them after the exchange. Maybe Radim would figure out where she was being held. "I'll call you afterward."

"What codes will you give them?" Radim asked when I dropped the phone in my pocket.

He meant, would I give them the ones Rio used, or the new ones that I created. "Rio wouldn't hand them over. She took a lot to keep them secret. If we give them hers, it might make things worse for her."

"Let me check with Maura," Radim said, pulling out his phone. "They'll go to Rio's office to use them. She will be in danger."

Again, he spoke in Czech. It made me wonder if I should trust him.

He ended the call. "She'll leave before we hand over the codes. She hasn't found anything big. Says it will take days to get more out of the data."

In days, more information wouldn't matter. Rio would either be safe or dead. "What should I do?"

"This is a trap, yes?" Radim grabbed his jacket from the hall. "They should be asking for money if our guess is right. If it is some low-level criminals, would they have the skills to use the data Rio found?"

"But they want it," I said. "I don't know why, and I don't care." I didn't say the words that flashed in my mind. *Maybe we were wrong. Maybe they were going to sell the passwords for money.*

"Give them all the codes, mix them up so it will take some time for them to work out which ones to use. Time will help. We must make a plan."

"What kind of plan?"

"Something that will keep you safe," Radim said. "You are going in there alone. If you get caught in the trap, I will need to rescue both of you."

"I don't need rescuing, remember?" I hoped I wouldn't anyway. "What plan?"

"I will be near, watching. I will set friends at the points where anyone can leave. We follow them to wherever they are keeping her, and we take Rio away from them."

"You make it sound simple," I said. "So many things can go wrong."

"They will go wrong whether we have a plan or not. Jack is paying you a lot of money, yes?"

"This is not about the money," I said. A flash of guilt must have shown on my face because he looked like he didn't believe me. "Yes. Jack is going to fund my future. I'm not going to put Rio at risk just to get paid."

"You would do this for free?" Radim sounded surprised.

"Probably. If Jack had pushed me harder."

He shrugged and then opened a hall closet and pulled out two motorcycle helmets. "Did you visit the Jewish Cemetery?"

"I might have walked by it, but I didn't pay attention to the area that much."

He handed me the blue helmet with snowflakes painted on it. "We go check it out. Then I make some calls, and then we will be ready for the hand over."

"Won't it be crowded with tourists?"

"Not this early."

Chapter 19

The cemetery was on all the tours, but right now the area was empty. When I looked it up before I came, the entrance looked like it was on a busy road, but Radim set me up on a small side street. The corner next to the museum turned so sharply that from a distance, it looked like a dead end. According to the sign on the door, the museum wouldn't open for an hour and I guess the shops didn't open unless foot traffic promised sales.

I stood with my back to the cemetery in front of the last of a row of stalls lining the right side of the street. Green shutters locked them down tight, but the stalls might be ready to open as the first tour group neared the area for all I knew. Small shops and a bakery lined the other side. I could tell there were people inside, but I stood alone, like a gunslinger at high noon waiting for the bad guy to draw. My nerves thrummed.

From my position, Radim was just visible around the turn waiting on his motorcycle, my helmet on his lap. He held his phone and pretended to be absorbed in something on the screen. He had three more people watching, but I had no idea where they were, or what they looked like.

"You have the codes?" a voice came from the stall beside me. They used one of those devices that changed the sound to a robotic voice.

"I want to know Rio is okay before I hand them over." I stepped closer, losing sight of Radim as I did.

"That is not the deal," the voice said. "Keep back."

I tried to see how someone would get in or out of the locked stall. There must be a way. No kidnapper was going to let themselves be trapped after getting what they wanted. Whoever spoke might have just arrived or been observing for hours, waiting for the right time.

"Do you have what we asked for?" the voice asked again.

"Yes." I clutched the paper with the codes in my pocket.

"Put it inside the gate."

"They're locked." Was someone inside waiting to take the message? If the museum was closed, how would they escape? I could see only a corner of the graveyard through the gates; headstones crowded every inch of ground.

"You don't need to open the gates. Place the document on the ground. Reach through."

"Is Rio still alive?" I didn't expect them to say no, but the more I delayed this handover the better. If they were here, they weren't beating Rio.

"Yes. Do as I said, or she will be closer to death."

"Prove she's alive. Her father won't pay for her body." I had no doubt about that.

"Wait."

I heard mumbling; a guy, and he was calling someone. That didn't fit my plan to stall them until we could act. If the man inside was alone, how did he plan to retrieve the paper when I left it inside the gate?

"If you don't leave the codes now, you will hear the girl's screams."

A bluff... I hoped. But at least it would tell me she wasn't dead. "If you don't give me proof she's alive, I'll walk away."

He muttered something again and then I heard Rio.

"Please help me," she sobbed. "Please tell my dad to pay whatever they want."

"Rio?" I called. If my voice carried enough, maybe she would feel safer.

"Yes." Sobbing again.

My mind boiled with the need to do something to help her. I took a step toward the stall.

"Stop," the altered voice said.

"Rio, we're going to rescue you," I said. "Soon. We're coming for you."

"Just do what they say," she said.

"Enough. She is alive. Put the codes through the gate."

I ran back to the building and slipped the paper on the ground. A closer glance inside showed crowded headstones filling a small space. No one waited to take it. I went back to the stall.

"How much money do you want?" I asked. If I got the ransom underway, I could get her away from them sooner.

"We will contact you."

"When?" I couldn't let him go.

"Just do as we say, and the girl will go free. She will be alive. If you don't follow instructions, she dies."

"How will you contact me?"

"Don't worry about that."

"I need to pull the money together. Tell me how much."

It was a losing battle, but I couldn't just walk away.

"Wait for instructions."

I tried to think of another way to stall them. I heard footsteps behind me. I turned, but no one was there. I ran back to the gates; the paper was gone, and still no one in sight. How could we follow them if we couldn't see them?

A few of the shops opened their doors, sending chimes into the silent street.

I moved to the stall, leaning against the shutter to look inside. The slats fitted too closely for that. "Tell me what to do next."

No answer. I managed to poke my finger in the crack between the shutters and create a sliver of a gap. All I saw was a speaker, no evidence that anyone had been there. The only person here was whoever took the paper.

I heard the motorcycle before I turned from the stall. Radim pulled up beside me and handed me the stupid snowflake helmet.

"They're gone," I said. "They were never here."

"Get on. One of my people watched a man leave the cemetery."

I hopped on the back. He tapped the side of my helmet and then his voice came through. "Tell me what they said."

Without the speakers I would have just been a passenger. We sped out of the street and turned toward Old Town Square.

"She's alive," I said. "In bad shape by the sound of it."

"You spoke to her?"

I told him everything as we wound around cars and growing crowds of tourists.

"If they wanted her codes, why didn't she hand them over?" He turned again and we were trapped beside a tour bus negotiating a corner. He cursed and swung us around the bus, barely missing colliding with a BMW.

"I haven't come up with anything more than our first guess," I said. "She found something so bad she was willing to die to protect it."

"But that was before you heard her. She said to give them everything, yes?"

I'd screwed up. I shouldn't have gotten so emotional. Radim knew our theory was broken and I'd ignored the facts. "Fuck!"

"Yes," he said. "Are you sure it was Rio?"

He turned wide onto the main road along the waterfront.

I thought back to what she'd said. Only a few words really and they were distorted by her tears. "It was a girl. That's all I'm sure of now."

"See that bike ahead? That's the man who took the paper."

"I guess part of the plan is working," I said. It didn't make me happy. Yes we had a lead, but we did nothing to make it happen.

"We follow him, yes. Let us hope he is returning to his partners, and not going somewhere to try to use the codes."

I kept quiet, leaving Radim to focus on our quarry. The not so little voice in my head was doing enough talking about how I'd made a mess of this; I didn't need him to add to the chorus.

"*Vinohrady*," Radim said.

"What?" I didn't recognize the word.

"He is going to *Vinohrady*. Not many places to hide a hostage there."

"That's good, right?" Maybe my mistake wouldn't cost

Rio her life. I'd only feel good about this when she was back with her dad, and I had a new identity.

"A bit."

I kept my eyes on the bike ahead of us. He didn't seem to know we were following, so it was not likely to be a trap. A lot of traffic headed up the hill with us. The rider had enough to do concentrating on avoiding accidents without looking back for a tail.

I felt our bike wobble.

Radim swore.

The tires squealed as they slipped out from under us.

I hit the ground; the bike skidded forward enough to avoid rolling over me. Radim lay a few feet away, face down on the sidewalk, not moving.

Chapter 20

It took seconds for my brain to send pain to me and when it did, I hurt all over. My hands burned; scrapes covered the palms, dirt and grit ground into the bloody mess. My jeans underneath me were shredded from the knees down, more blood staining them. Aches and throbs along my legs and side promised spectacular bruises, but I could wiggle my fingers and toes without passing out, so nothing broken.

I couldn't stay down. If Radim was hurt, I needed to find help. Rio still had to be saved, but I only had the capacity to deal with one disaster at a time. I rolled onto my side and struggled to stand, using my elbows for leverage to save my hands. I staggered a little before straightening up, confirming the lack of fractures.

I could breathe. I could walk. The rest of it could be dealt with by showering, Band-Aids, and fresh clothes.

Nothing on the road gave me a clue about what happened. People hurried toward us from a bus stop a few feet away. I made it to Radim's side just as he groaned and rolled over. His right arm flopped, and his shoulder hung too low. Dislocated. If that was the worst of his injuries, we were lucky.

"How bad?" I asked.

Then people speaking Czech surrounded us.

"English?" I didn't have the patience to do anything else.

"Do you need an ambulance?" a woman asked, holding out her phone.

I looked at Radim.

"*Ne, děkuji,*" he said.

"Is that yes or no?" I asked.

"No." He rolled into a sitting position. "Can you put this back in?"

"I will call the police," the helpful woman said. "I saw what happened. They shouldn't get away with such things. These rich kids with big cars."

"It's okay," I said. "We need to go." I knelt beside Radim and told him I knew how to put his shoulder back into place.

"Can you identify the car?" Radim asked. "I remember it was black."

"I took a picture," the woman said. She touched her phone and handed it to me.

A black Mercedes. At least I wasn't looking at a photo of the accident; I didn't need to see exactly what happened right now. "Please send this to me. For when we call the police."

My words seemed to assure her that someone would be punished. I gave her my phone number. She sent it. "I added my contact information," she said. Then she went back to join the other people who had drifted back to the bus stop.

"This is going to hurt," I said.

"I have done this before."

"How many times?" The more often he'd dislocated it, the more likely it would slip out again until the joint fully healed.

"Two," he said.

I got into position, trying not to jostle the arm. Knowing I had an audience didn't help, nor did the pressure on my scraped skin. I looked over at the people who'd come to assist us earlier. Their bus arrived and they stopped looking at me.

"Okay, on three," I said. "One, two." Then I popped the joint back into place.

Radim dealt with the pain by cradling his arm and swearing for a full minute. I sat back, leaning on my hands until they reminded me of the damage.

"What next?" I asked.

"The bike?"

I walked over. The bike was too heavy for me to lift, but everything looked whole and unbent. "Should work."

"Can you ride?"

"Not one that size."

He used his left hand to place a call. A few words I couldn't understand and then he disconnected. "Someone will pick us up."

"Maybe I should start learning Czech," I said. "I can't rely on someone translating for me when I live here."

"You know how to order beer, and now you know how to say 'no thank you.'"

I laughed. It bordered on hysterical in my ears. Between losing our possible connection to Rio and the trauma of the crash, I was close to the edge of my control. "I can practice those for a while."

Radim's friend dropped us off at my hotel. Radim had been wearing appropriate clothes. So now that his shoulder was in place, he just had a few scrapes on his hand to suffer, unless we got into a fight.

I dug into my suitcase for the first aid kit. I tossed him an alcohol wipe and some Band-Aids and then took the kit into the bathroom. I washed the grit out of my hands and then checked my legs. My left leg was fine; my right leg took most of the damage. I slipped out of my jeans and chucked them toward the tiny garbage container.

I tried to wash the dirt from my shin and calf in the sink, but it was too high and too small. I stripped and got in the shower. When I was clean, free of grit and over the stinging agony, I used the alcohol wipes to sanitize the wounds. I didn't have anything big enough to cover the scrape, so I smeared on some antibiotic cream and wrapped myself in a towel.

"I need some clothes," I said by way of warning as I came out of the bathroom.

Radim was talking on his phone. He turned away when he saw me step out of the bathroom. I grabbed an outfit and went back to dress. It took some lip biting to pull the jeans on through the agony in my hands and leg. I persevered and was dressed and back in the room as soon as I was decent. The pain would subside, and I hoped that the cream would stop my jeans from sticking to the wounds.

"Okay," I said. "What next?"

"The university?" Radim said. "They must go there to use the codes."

"What about the motorcycle?"

"We were the only ones chasing it." Radim grabbed the first aid kit. "You have painkillers?"

I found the bottle of Advil in my suitcase and tossed it to him. He took two and told me to do the same.

"How sure are you that they were going to *Vinohrady*?"

"Why would they go that way otherwise? They didn't know we were following."

"Do you think it was an accident?" I agreed that the rider on the other motorcycle didn't seem aware we chased them, but what if they had? "Could they have made us crash, and called for that car?"

"It's possible. Give me your phone."

I unlocked it and brought up the picture. "Can you find someone to identify the owner?"

"Yes, but unless we know the owner is a criminal, the identity won't help. And maybe it was stolen. And probably they will say that."

I didn't need to follow up on the accident unless there was a connection. The driver was getting a pass on this one. "We should find out, or at least try."

He sent the text to another of his contacts.

"Can you walk to the university?" he asked as he passed my phone back.

"As long as I don't have to rush," I said. "Did you talk to Petr?"

"I left a message."

The day already felt like it had run its course and it was only ten AM. We got coffee and a pastry on the way. The sugar and caffeine helped a little. A big glass of wine would have been better, but that would come later to celebrate Rio's freedom — or drown my guilt at failing.

We walked in the front door of the university. Students walked around the lobby or sat talking in groups. More like I expected this time. Radim sent another text to Petr to meet us in Rio's office.

When we got there, the room looked about the same. The desk was still pushed aside, so no one had moved it since Maura left. The pile of printouts was spread on the floor in the corner just the way Radim had left them.

"We can't just wait in here," I said. "We need to trap them inside."

Petr joined us before I could elaborate.

"You don't look good," he said. "What happened?"

"A story to be told over a beer," Radim said. "Has anyone been here?"

"Your friend in the wheelchair left over an hour ago," Petr said. "No one has been inside, but two men tried to get in."

"Where are they?" I wondered if the university had a holding area, or if the police had come.

"Security sent them away," Petr said. "Should I have arranged to let them in?"

"No. They should not have access," Radim said, "until we can observe."

"Did you get a description?" I asked. If we knew what they looked like, maybe it would help.

"Two men, maybe twenty-five, maybe thirty. One blond, one dark. Radim's height. Skinny." Petr rattled off the details like he was reading them from a police file.

"How do you know? Did you talk to security? We should talk to them," I said.

"Gossip travels fast in a small community," Petr said. "I can arrange for the security guard to come if you like."

"That would be good," Radim said. "We will leave this room unlocked, Petr. When these men come back, we will be watching."

"Are you sure they will try?" Petr asked.

"They need what's in here," I said. "They will definitely be back."

"Then we must tell the security team not to stop them," Petr said. "Come, there is a good place for you to watch the door."

He led us past some students at open desks to another

office. This one had no door, a desk, a couple of chairs, and a computer. The open doorway faced Rio's room and had enough distance that no one would suspect they were being watched. "It may take some time for the security guards to come."

"No problem," I said. "I don't think they'll be back right away."

When Petr left us, Radim sat at the desk. "This is going to be difficult."

"I don't relish sitting here for hours either. What else can we do?" I needed something other than my injuries to focus on. Something to move us a few steps closer to Rio since there was no guarantee we could get answers from whoever showed up here.

Radim shrugged. "The university will have maps of the city. We can look at the area where the texts came from."

Unless he suddenly had a memory of a torture room in one of the buildings, I didn't hold out hope. Following a fresher lead would be better. "What's in *Vinohrady*? Are there some maps we can look at? Maybe you can figure out where they're keeping her?"

Radim pulled the keyboard closer. He typed and grunted. "Her login works here."

I gritted my teeth against the pain and moved one of the chairs next to him. "I guess it will pass the time. Can you see her door?"

"Yes." He entered a search. "*Vinohrady* is not what it was. Now it is a popular place for young families. But like most of Prague, the area has secrets."

He brought up a street map and told me to keep an eye on Rio's office.

Radim stared at the screen, occasionally typing or clicking. Staring at the room across the way was straining my ability to stay awake. Jet lag was no longer the problem. I'd been awake too long, and my injuries were draining what little strength I had left. Band-Aids and cream were not the only things I pulled out of my case when we were at the hotel. I had the No-Doze.

Taking one would keep me alert, but what would it do to my decision making? "How are you doing?" I asked, just to avoid working out an acceptable answer.

"If I was looking for a place to hold someone, and what I needed to do would be noisy, there are a few near where we crashed."

Knowing we had some locations to search lifted me for a moment. "And how much pain are you in?"

"I can still do what we need," he said. "Come, let me show you what I found."

I positioned myself beside him in a way that allowed me to see part of the door to Rio's office. I would notice if it opened, but probably not who went in.

He had three buildings on the screen. All apartments and all looking pretty expensive. "No broken-down hovels?"

"Not in *Vinohrady*," he said. "But these are old and will have basements. It is perhaps like the last one."

"So, we can slip in without anyone noticing? A concierge with loose ethics?"

"It will require some work to see if we can get in." He pointed at the first one. "This building was a popular place for the Secret Police to meet. I think it's probably been used for interrogation."

He pointed to the next one. "One of the people I knew lived here after he made sure his father-in-law was arrested."

"He turned in his own father-in-law?"

"It was a bad time."

It still didn't look like a place you could wander into and check out the sinister rooms in the basement. "And the third?"

"I think I was there," he said.

"You don't know?" I looked over toward Rio's office remembering my role as observer.

"I was blindfolded. Things happened. I cannot be sure."

"How confident are you that one of these is the right place?" I heard footsteps headed our way. "Is it near the area Michael sent us?"

"If we are right about them going back to Rio when they had the codes, these are the only buildings I think would work. The texts came from a different part of the city."

"You wanted to talk to me?" A security guard stood in our doorway, blocking my view of Rio's door.

"Yes," Radim said, waving him into the room.

"About the men who tried to break into the room?" He cocked his head toward Rio's office.

"We think they are trying to steal her work," Radim said.

I let him do the talking while I kept my eye on the room across the way. I popped one of the pills while his attention was elsewhere.

"Tell me what happened," Radim said.

"You are police?"

"We are protecting Rio Hennessey."

"How do I know that is true?"

"Her father engaged us," I said to short cut the negotiations for his cooperation. "I can call him for you."

The guard paled and said involving a patron was unnecessary. Jack's money finally working in my favor. "So, will you tell us?"

He thought my question over for a moment, then started reporting. "Two men attempted to force the lock on the door. I was called by one of the students to stop them. My partner and I escorted the two men from the building and added them to the list of people who are not allowed inside."

His delivery was stilted, but most reporting language was. It didn't help that he was speaking English for my benefit.

The caffeine started buzzing in my veins. I fidgeted with coins in my pocket to hide the effect.

"Can you describe them?" Radim asked.

"Tall. I would say, one hundred eight-five centimeters. One was blond. One had dark hair. They both had bad skin like teenagers. The blond one was hurt, possibly a bruised rib. The dark haired one was clearly in charge."

"Names?" Radim asked.

"They refused."

"You noticed a lot of details," I said.

"I was a policeman," he said. "It is my training. Mr. Zalic said we were to let them enter if they returned."

"We'll be following them when they leave. They can't get into her files and do damage." I hoped I was right about that. Maybe we'd been at a disadvantage. Maybe Rio had told them what to look for.

A radio crackled and someone said a word I didn't recognize.

The security guard stood. "They are here. I will be close if you need help."

Chapter 21

I sat beside Radim, pretending to look at the screen. If the kidnappers turned our way, I hoped we would pass as mature students deep in our work and unaware of our surroundings. "I guess it's unlikely they'll speak English," I said. "You'll have to get close."

"Should I also record them so I can remember to tell you everything?" He grinned at me. "Don't worry so much that you can't understand the language."

I was happy he could still feel some joy at what we were doing. On the whole, this was a huge step forward, so a little of the worry lifted from me. "I just need the highlights."

The two men leaned casually next to the door, pretending to chat. The blond took what looked like a small drill from his pocket; a lock pick gun. A high-end one; these two had picked locks before. The other students had vacated the floor quietly after the security guard suggested it was time to leave. That meant no one would hear the noise of the tool, or of whatever we needed to do to gain a lead.

"We should be glad they don't want to break the door down," I said. "If they thought they'd find what they wanted fast, I'm sure that's what would happen."

The door opened and both men went inside, not bothering to close it; another piece of luck.

Radim beckoned me to follow him. We stopped just short of the room. I crouched under a desk, pulling the chair to stop anyone noticing me. Radim flattened himself against the wall next to the door. This all felt a bit like a cartoon.

The two men talked. Their voices grew louder after a few minutes. I guessed they'd tried the wrong combination of all the passwords. Good!

Radim stepped away from the door and rushed to our office. I held my breath, fighting the urge to run as the two stormed out of the room yelling at each other. When the sound of their voices faded enough that I was sure we would be safe, I crawled out from under the desk, my hands making me pay for pressing them on the carpet.

Radim met me as I stood.

"Not *Vinohrady*," he said. "Rio is not there. One of the bosses, I think. The rider was going for orders."

"Did they happen to mention an address?" If we were on a roll of good luck, I wanted as much as the universe offered.

"Just a few clues that most people wouldn't notice. There are only two places where they might be holding her. Both are within walking distance."

"Is your shoulder going to be a problem?" I asked as I started toward the front door. "We need to move fast."

"I will not slow us down," he said. "How are your wounds?"

"Sore. I'll cope."

He didn't say anything else, but I got the impression he wanted to know why I wasn't falling asleep on my feet. That might have been my own guilt about the pills rather than the effect of a hit of caffeine.

The two men slipped through the doors as we entered the lobby. I hurried forward to see which direction they took. "They are going toward the side entrance."

Radim tugged me back. "It will be faster if we go through inside."

We ran to the side door and out to the street. I had the training not to get too close to someone I was tailing. We couldn't lose sight of the kidnappers by being cautious. Having all the tourists around would help; not knowing my surroundings as well as I usually do wouldn't.

Radim pulled me to a stop as I started to cross the road. "Wait, look."

The two kidnappers were strolling toward us, their argument forgotten. I turned away as if I was speaking to Radim but kept them in my peripheral line of sight.

"How far apart are these two buildings?" I wondered if we would gain a clue when they turned a corner. Something we could use to get ahead of them. I had the strong feeling that Rio was going to take the brunt of their earlier anger.

"Only a few streets," Radim said.

The two turned right.

We hurried to the corner. I got there first and glanced down to see them hop on a motorcycle — probably the same one as before. "Fuck."

Radim grabbed my arm and pulled me back. "They are not going to the house where they keep Rio."

"Why? We've been just guessing for hours. Tell me what makes you so sure."

"They wouldn't need a motorcycle to get to either of them. Come," he said and started down the street he just pulled me out of. "Parking at any of these buildings would bring attention."

"So? They might just be riding to some place nearby and then walking in."

"It doesn't make sense to do that," Radim said. "We are only a few streets from the first one, an abandoned train station. We can go around the back and avoid being seen."

Since I didn't have a better plan, I let him lead. It took five minutes to walk to our destination. The station was completely boarded up, and the city had put up a fence to keep people out. I couldn't see any way of getting in without being observed, especially with a kidnapped girl.

"Come on," Radim said. He continued walking while I stood gawping. He led me to the corner of the fencing, looked around and pulled a section aside. "Go in."

Just inside the fence was a small door into the building. I yanked at the handle and it came open just wide enough for us to squeeze through. "They must have come at night if she's here," I said, then remembered how bad Rio looked; they wouldn't have had a choice. "Maybe that's why they didn't come straight here."

Radim didn't answer. He was poking into corners and tapping on the walls. I stepped around a moldy, stained mattress and joined him. "Hidden panel?"

"I think so."

It was pretty clear that vagrants had squatted here recently. "How would they keep everything they were doing quiet if people can get inside so easily?"

"It is not hard to discourage visitors."

Radim looked up at the ceiling and then along the side of the wall. He kicked at the rotting baseboard and I heard a click. A door silently swung open two feet from me. Whoever created the entrance had done a great job of reinforcing everything.

"So, this mess is just for show?" I followed Radim in, kicking a chunk of fallen plaster into place to block the door from closing. He put his finger to his lips and started walking into the dark.

I couldn't hear anything ahead of us. But inside was dry and the floor was even, and I couldn't smell mildew, toilets, or rotting food.

That didn't mean it was pleasant. The floor was littered with rubble; in the dim light it was a hazard and slowed me down. Radim wasn't having much better luck, but he had his hands to help him balance. I was not putting my hands on the wall without gloves.

"How far?" I asked, keeping my voice low.

"I haven't been here before. Maybe we are tunneling under the road, but I don't really think so. Too much risk of a cave-in."

"It's getting darker," I said. The light from the open door had already faded to nothing.

"You want to wait?"

"No." If he was willing to keep going, I refused to be the weak link. I pulled out my phone. "Can we use the light from this?"

Radim considered his answer. "Point it down to the floor."

I aimed just ahead of him. The pool of light didn't spread far enough to help me, so I moved as close to him as possible. I would still need to remember what was on the ground, but I would be fine. Or as fine as I could be when we were creeping down a tunnel toward the unknown. If we needed to run out, it would be another story.

The tunnel ended in a T. To the right was a stretch of

clear floor with a blank wall at the end. The left hand of the T was only a foot or so long before leading to a door.

"Wait," Radim said. He took off to the right and tapped the wall and then came back. "Sometimes there is a false one. This time not."

We stood in front of the door. It looked heavy but I saw nothing reinforcing the wood. There was a normal key lock and no contact points for an alarm system. That didn't mean there wasn't one.

Radim picked the lock, then pulled the door open. Inside was the same as the last room we'd hoped to find Rio in. A chair, bare walls, blood on the floor. The only difference was the blood. It was clearly too old to be Rio's.

"So, the next house?" I asked. "We're getting closer."

"I hope," Radim said. "I don't like being in this position. I normally know everything I need. This delving into other people's past is... uncomfortable."

When we were outside the door, Radim pushed it closed. The door swung an inch toward us. He pressed it closed again and it swung open again. "It will take too long to lock," he said. "The next person to come here will think twice about security."

"We don't know if we tripped any alarms." I didn't care if the next person who wanted to use this room worried about security, but maybe it would stop them doing horrible things to someone. We weren't interfering with a kid's birthday party, after all. Unless it was tonight, I would be long gone and Radim could look after himself.

I stumbled a couple of times on the way out but managed not to do any more damage to myself. We slipped into the main room. Radim kicked the plaster doorstop aside and the hidden door swung closed. He tapped the baseboard into place.

"How far to the next place?"

Something moved in the corner. I turned and saw a bundle of rags and hair coming at me.

I felt Radim move into position at my side. "We're leaving," I yelled.

I knew this vagrant couldn't understand me, but I couldn't stop the words. The homeless guy kept coming.

Radim said something in Czech and then picked up a piece of rebar stuck in a clump of bricks. I bent my knees and put my shoulder forward to take the brunt of the rush. He was only protecting his squat. I didn't want to hurt him.

He barreled into me. Radim swung his weapon, contacting with the guy's back to no effect through the layers of clothing. He was behind us now. We had a clear path to the door — if you didn't count the mattress and the debris.

The guy turned and I saw fear and determination. He was moving his weight from side to side, deciding on who was the best target.

"Run," I said.

We were outside leaning against the closed door. I felt like I'd raced in a hundred-meter sprint. Radim was gasping beside me.

"We won't win if there's a fight ahead of us," I said.

"We need weapons. Guns. I know someone," he said. His hand on his damaged shoulder.

"Is it out again?" I reached over to check.

"No." He flinched away from my hand.

"Guns aren't a good idea," I said. "I'm not sure I could hold one right now."

He got control of his breathing and stopped rubbing his injury. "You don't need to hold a weapon. I can."

"With your shoulder? After one shot, I'll have to put your joint back in."

"Then what do you suggest?"

"We try to do it without a fight." He started to argue, and I held up my hand to stop him. "Yeah, I'm aware we are not likely to avoid one. Is the next place like this one?"

"Probably."

"Then there will be lots of things on the floor for us to use."

"It was not useful in there."

"That wasn't a real fight. They won't be padded with extra clothes. On the other hand, we'll have more adrenaline." I tried to sound like I believed my words. "Will they have guns?"

"It's possible. This isn't like America, but they are available."

"Good to know." Why did I ask? I still wasn't willing to take the time to get one. I told myself it was because of our injuries, but I'd never liked them. Too final and too easy to shoot the wrong person.

My phone buzzed in my pocket. "Jack." I said when I saw the text. "They've contacted him for the ransom, finally."

"Perhaps they abandoned their plan with the data?"

"It does seem like convenient timing. He says they want ten million in diamonds. He's arranged for us to pick up the package in an hour."

"Where?"

I showed him the address. "That is the bank beside the university. Jack has good connections."

"Does ten million sound like enough?" I would have asked for more, but maybe the kidnappers had a deadline we didn't know about.

"It's a lot. And perhaps it is low enough that no one will come after them. Where do we deliver this ransom?"

I asked Jack. *They'll contact me in two hours. Don't lose the diamonds. Wait for my next text.*

"How are we supposed to get into the bank?" I realized that was something Jack could answer better than Radim. I sent the text.

Code is 225731.

"How confident should we be about getting Rio back?" I asked Radim.

"If we hand over their money? I would give fifty percent odds on them freeing her. But we know that she may have seen them or heard enough to identify them. I am being generous."

"Even if they let her go, do you think they might put up a fight?"

"No reason to do that," he said. "Too easy to lose the ransom, to get caught."

I knew he had no more information than I did. I just didn't trust my decision making right now. My gut said to keep looking for her. We had an hour before the ransom would be ready and probably an hour and a half before we ran out of time to pick it up.

We knew of one more place that they might be holding her. If we waited to pick up the diamonds, we risked losing an opportunity to rescue Rio without paying. If we didn't wait, her kidnappers might decide she was expendable.

"You want to go to the next building?" Radim asked. "We should go now. If we save Jack the money, maybe he will share some?"

"Jack's not that generous," I said, "but I don't want to wait around for an hour, and then longer if they take their time with the location."

"Okay," Radim said. He pulled away from the door and pointed at the fence. "Let's go."

Part of me wanted him to try to talk me out of it. But moving was close enough to progress, so I sent a text to Jack. *I'll be waiting.* Then I turned off the phone so I wouldn't spend our time arguing with him.

It wasn't even noon and I was tired enough to have lived a whole day.

Chapter 22

"It's not abandoned," I said. The building looked solid and I imagined it would be simple to soundproof any of the rooms that might leak a scream or two. A woman entered about two minutes after we arrived, and she triggered motion sensor floodlights. "Pretty high security."

"This is a government building," Radim said as if it didn't matter. "There will be a guard."

"You could have mentioned that before," I said. "Do you really think they're keeping her in a file room, or is the government used to having kidnapped Canadian teenagers beaten in the conference room?"

"Not now, but this has been a government building for a long time." He started walking toward the front door. "It has not always been used for offices."

I grabbed his arm. "We can't just go in," I hissed. He might not worry, but I had all kinds of disasters running through my head. How would we escape if the kidnappers stopped us? If they had guns, would some security guard come to our rescue? "What is the plan here?"

"I need something from inside. This is not where we

are going to look for her. I cannot get access to that place without a key from this one."

"The kidnappers received permission to be there," I said. "Or did they need a key to hold Rio hostage and brutalize her?"

He looked down at me and I realized he expected me to just follow. He should know I wouldn't do that.

"You need to tell me the plan."

"I will go into the office and get permission to enter a small outbuilding not far from here. I will tell them I am working with a private university to arrange for students to inspect the old architecture."

"And they'll just believe you?" It was a pretty good plan now that I understood that we didn't need to go into the bowels of a government building.

He pulled a card out of his pocket. "I have this."

Credentials for Rio's university.

"When did you get that?"

"How do you know I haven't always had it?" He grinned. "Petr gave it to me the first time we met him."

"Will it be enough?" I imagined this kind of thing needed some advance notice and some applications and background checks.

"I also have this." He held out a wad of euros.

"And what will I be doing?" I knew better than to berate him for not including me. Or telling me what he was going to do without me.

"Waiting in that coffee shop." He pointed to a Costa Coffee twenty meters down the street.

"It's only an hour before the deadline to pick up the ransom," I said.

"Yes."

I waited for him approach the building before I went to the coffee shop. The first time we worked separately when we were actually following a lead, and my job was to sit on a stool and wait. I ordered an espresso and a muffin and sat at the window.

I thought we were working as a team. I'd even started to trust him, but now, suddenly he'd withdrawn, no more jokes, no more volunteering information. It had been a long night, and maybe I missed the way these searches had affected him. Maybe too many memories had piled up. I remembered how I wanted to crawl into a dark space and push everyone away in the aftermath of beating Vince.

I had no other choice. Or that's what Jack told me at the time. He had a client on trial for his life, an innocent one — of course, he lied. My job was to find another reasonable suspect. I did that.

If one experience affected me so deeply that I had to run away from my life, what would multiple instances do? I got the strong feeling Radim had been on both sides of that torture chair.

Ten minutes later I saw him walking toward me. I tossed back the last of my coffee and went to join him on the street.

"Did it work?"

He held out a key. "This has to be returned in two hours."

"That should be enough," I said. "The ransom deadline will run out before that. How hidden is this place?" I wished for a little darkness now.

"There are trees, and it is away from the street. No one will pay attention to us going in. If we come out with Rio, we don't care who sees, yes?"

He had a point. "Let's go."

"We need some things," he said.

"No guns," I told him.

"Yes, I heard you the first time you made that decision.

We need water. I need to eat something. We need painkillers."

"Your arm?" I had barely noticed my hands, but now that he mentioned pain, I felt the dry crust of scabs pulling at my skin. And I knew it wouldn't take much to turn them into little blobs of agony. "I could use some gloves."

"Get water and meet me back here," he said. Without another word, he headed across the street to a pharmacy.

Costa Coffee, like Starbucks, sold bottled water. I got three.

Radim crossed the road to join me when I left the coffee shop. He handed me a bag filled with latex gloves, a power bar, and a bottle of the Czech version of Advil. "This way." He led me down a side street that curved a few feet in.

"Wait. I thought it was on the grounds of that building."

"No, but it's not far. Give me some of the pain medicine." He took one of the water bottles and downed two of the pills and the power bar. "Put on the gloves and take a few of them."

"Stop ordering me around," I said as I followed his commands.

"Why three?" he asked, taking the bag from me.

"Rio," I said.

He waited until I put on two pairs of the gloves, one to protect my hands and one to catch any blood that might seep through, I guess. He watched me down three Advil.

"Finish the water," he said.

When I did, he tossed the bag into a trash can. "She will receive what she needs from the hospital."

Maybe I was the one with the problem, but if he couldn't get over whatever was bothering him, we would be in trouble. "Why are you being such an asshole?"

"We don't have time to argue," he said. "Let's go."

"No. What changed?"

He stared at me long enough to make me squirm. Then he looked away. "I saw you taking something. I don't work with people who need drugs."

Oh. "Nothing," I said. "Caffeine pills. I've been awake a long time."

"Are there more?" he asked.

"Yes." I pulled the bottle from my pocket.

He grabbed it and tossed it in the trash. "No more. Or I leave you to this job alone."

I wanted to tell him that I was an adult and capable of making my own decisions and that I could find Rio on my own. But even in my caffeinated mind the argument sounded about as far from a professional investigator as you can get. And I had no clue what to do without him. "Okay. Let's go."

We worked our way through a warren of twists and double backs. I lost my sense of direction after we turned into an alley that I would have sworn was the entrance to a garage. It ended in a tiny park, trees almost obscuring the house inside.

"Won't people wonder why we're going in?" I asked. A few people hung out smoking in doorways.

"They won't care." Radim took my arm and we walked into the shade.

At least I had my bit of darkness.

The structure was more of a hut; brick walls, no windows, slate roof. The door was dark wood with iron braces. "What was this for?"

"Guard house," Radim said as he slid in the key. "The river is not far. You will see."

The inside of the building was no more welcoming than the outside. I guess that was the point. Bare bricks and solid wooden floors, no ceiling, just the underside of the roof. Dim light bled in through gaps in the tiles, even less through the door. In the shadow at the back I barely made out a trap door.

"Phone," Radim said as he swung the door closed.

I turned mine on and tapped the flashlight. It illuminated a bird's nest in the far corner and a curtain of cobwebs. "This was what I imagined all along," I said. "Although the details are worse than anything my brain could dredge up. I guess we're going down?"

"I don't know the other way," Radim said. "We could find it when we leave, but another way will empty out to the river."

He lifted the trapdoor, grunting as the weight transferred to his shoulder. "I'll go first," he said. "Remember to keep the light facing down."

He sat on the edge of the hole and then twisted around as he found stairs. I stepped forward and peeked inside before doing the same. A narrow set of steps led into the darkness. "How did they manage to bring Rio down?"

"I would have drugged her," he said. "Then she can't fight. It is easy to make a body look like a package."

We went down the equivalent of two floors by my guess. The air was damp, and things scurried away as we approached. Rats favored the river and the thought didn't make me feel any better about being here. I started to understand the way claustrophobes reacted.

I controlled my breathing to avoid going down that track. Rio needed me alert and calm, not climbing the walls to escape.

While I paused for control, Radim kept walking. He disappeared into the dark corridor, then reappeared.

"If you are not going to come with me, give me your

phone. I need the light and I want to save the battery in mine."

"I'm coming," I said. He didn't need to know why I stopped, and I reminded myself that this time the asshole behavior was probably his reaction to the place, not to me.

It was hard to judge the distance underground, but we stumbled on for five minutes. Up top that would have been much farther than down here. Unless I was completely disoriented, we were going in the direction of the river. I sped up to tap Radim on the shoulder and signal him to stop.

Sound would carry, so I put my lips against his ear and asked, "Are there rooms down here?"

"Dungeons," he whispered into my ear. "We are getting close. They kept people here in ancient times so when they died it was easy to roll the body into the river."

I stepped back and nodded for him to continue forward. He took a few steps then stopped and beckoned to me.

Faint sounds of talking came from ahead. And light. I shut down my phone.

Radim took my hand and placed it on his back and started creeping forward. My sight was limited because I'd lost my night vision to the flashlight. I had to trust him to be sure when we were near enough.

Another ten steps and I recognized the sounds as two men; the cadence and occasional raised voice confirmed they were arguing. Unfortunately, my Czech hadn't improved in the last hour.

We were so close that the light coming from the room was sufficient to see my surroundings again. The door to what I assumed was a dungeon cell stood open only a few steps away.

Radim drew me against the wall. He leaned forward a little to hear better.

While I waited for the interpretation, I scanned the area for things to use as weapons. No luck. This was the least damaged of all the places we'd looked for her. Unfortunately, there seemed to be nowhere to hide if the men came out.

Radim nudged me back down the corridor until we were far enough away to whisper.

"They are holding her here," Radim said. "The argument is about what to do with Rio. One wants to leave her to die, the other says the boss won't like it if they did. That he'll punish them, maybe take away their cut."

"I wish we knew if it was just them," I said. "It's going to be hard to get her away from two men and then we have to run back along this tunnel with a wounded girl."

"I heard no other voice," Radim said. "I don't know how far in they are, but we can't risk looking in unless we're ready to fight."

"Fists against guns isn't going to work."

"That's all we have," he said. Did I hear a hint of blame in his tone? "We need to see around that corner."

"Isn't it a cell?"

"No, the entrance to a group of cells. The guard would sit at the opening. It will be like a jail. Cells lining the walls."

"Do you have your phone?" I pulled mine out and he handed his to me.

"Okay. We keep mine in reserve in case this all goes sideways." I had him unlock his phone and found the camera. "It isn't my first time at this." I meant my words to reassure him before I told him what I was going to do. I left out the part that every other time there had been a signal so I could transmit the recording. Of course, there wasn't one down here.

"If we look in, they'll probably see us no matter how low we go, or how quick we are. But they might not notice, or they might dismiss the phone as a rat, if we slide it along the floor to video the interior."

"It does not look like a rat," he helpfully pointed out.

"Not yet." I slipped off my jacket, tied a knot in the sleeve, tucking the phone into the folds of the knot. I tested it by taking a couple of frames of video and made an adjustment to clear the lens from the fabric. "One fake rat."

Chapter 23

"How are you going to push it into place?" Radim asked.

I wished I had a stick, but we work with what we have. I set it to record. "It doesn't need to go far."

I slipped back to the entrance to the cells and lay on the floor as close as I could to the opening. Ignoring the damp and smell of mildew, I put my arm inside the sleeve and extended my reach until the camera had a view into the room. I counted to twenty and then slowly pulled the phone back, doing my best to mimic a rat sniffing for crumbs.

When I rejoined Radim, he dragged me farther away so we could talk a little louder. I stopped recording and freed the phone from my jacket as we went.

We crowded over the screen; I moved the playback until I could see the wall.

The video didn't quite get a full view, but what we had lifted my spirits from the basement. Two men, and no indication that there was anyone else. They stood in the center of a square space, and just past them I could make out another passage, and another light source.

"If we surprise them, we might be able to grab Rio." I ran the video again as I spoke, hoping to notice another detail, maybe something that would help us get in and take her without getting us killed.

"How will you incapacitate them?" Radim pointed at the screen. "Maybe one of the chairs?"

"I'd prefer them to be conscious. At least one. We need to know who this boss is. Did they say anything that might lead us to him? Was it a him?"

"Yes, a man," Radim said. "It would be better to hit hard. We can get Rio and then interrogate these two."

"It has to be her, right?" I asked. "We're working on faith that they don't have a regular habit of kidnapping girls?"

"We won't know until we go in. Are you worried that they will be able to stop us?"

I was. The chairs looked flimsy. It would be better if the men were gone, or at least one of them. But as far as I could see, to leave they needed to come past us. "Do you think we could get across the opening? If we could avoid standing between them and the exit, we might be able to outwait them. They'll have to leave to pick up the ransom."

"Good idea. They left her alone to come to the university, so they don't seem worried about Rio escaping on her own. It means she's tied up."

In the video, the two men faced away from the doorway. "It's a risk if it isn't her. What did they say exactly?"

"They called her the... bitch is the English version. They didn't talk about diamonds, or codes or mention her name." He glanced at the time on the phone. "If we waste more time, we won't get to the bank before the deadline."

"Yeah, I think they'll be demanding delivery as soon as we pick them up. Jack must be frantic since he can't get me." How much was I willing to gamble? It had to be everything. "I don't think we have a choice, right? If it's not Rio, it's still some poor girl who needs rescuing."

"Okay," Radim said. "I will look first. If the way is clear, I will signal you and you must not hesitate. When you are past the door, I will follow. If the way is not clear, do we go in and fight?"

I grinned at his optimism. "How's your shoulder? If you keep popping it out, you'll need surgery to fix it."

"I will protect it." He pointed at my hands. "Will you be able to pick up a weapon?"

"Probably. It will only hurt until I put it down, right?"

Once again, we crept toward the light shining from the cells. Radim pressed his back into the wall just in front of the opening. He cocked his head, listening to a conversation that had cooled in the moments we'd been gone. He turned his head slowly around the corner and then back, pointing to me to move.

I held my breath and sped past, not looking inside so I could preserve some of my vision for when the light was dimmer and hoping that I wouldn't trip. It was dark only a few feet behind where I stopped. The air was damper and smelled of river.

Radim looked at me and shook his head.

Why didn't we think about getting separated? He had nowhere to hide and we couldn't communicate. I flexed my hands getting ready to punch or throw a chair.

Radim held up his hand, leaned again to glance in and kept moving until he was behind me. He plucked at my jacket and walked into the dark.

When we were far enough away from the door to talk again, he leaned in to whisper into my ear. "Rio must be in a cell. I saw them walking toward one."

The cold was starting to seep from the stone wall into

my bones. The river must be only a few yards away. It wouldn't take long before either of us was too stiff to fight. "Do we move now?"

"The same plan, I think," he said. "If they haven't moved in half an hour, we go in. Okay?"

As much as I wanted this over, I knew we had to work the odds. Waiting was less risky than charging in, until something changed. "Fifteen minutes," I said. "Any longer and I don't think I will be in any condition to fight."

We didn't have to wait even that long. About five minutes later, just as my fingers were getting numb, the two men left, walking toward the trap door. As soon as their flashlight dimmed, I moved toward the cell. Radim stepped around me to enter first, as if I needed protecting.

I was thankful that the lights were still on. This was not a place to explore in the dark, and my phone didn't have much charge in it. At the front, the roof was a little over six feet. Low, but at least we could stand. A few steps in, the roof slanted down until we had to walk bent over, beyond that were more cells.

The first two were empty, well, if you didn't count the rat nests and dead vermin. Neither were roomier than the walkway we stood in. That fact didn't relieve my claustrophobia. It just made me glad I wasn't inside a cell.

I took another step and the lights went out with a click. "Fuck!"

"Close your eyes," Radim whispered from ahead. "Let them adjust."

"I know how to deal with this." I couldn't count on there being enough ambient light for me to see when they adjusted but I did squeeze them shut. "You think they are on a timer?"

"Did you see any switches on the way down?" He placed his hand on my shoulder.

"It's too soon for them to be outside," I said. "And no, we didn't see any switches or wires."

I opened my eyes and saw each cell was lit with a dim light. "What the hell?"

"In the ground above," Radim said. "The opening let people throw garbage down onto the prisoner. It kept the air clean, too."

I imagined that garbage wasn't the only thing to find its way down the shaft. "Keep moving," I said.

A few steps forward and there was Rio in one of the middle cells. She was gagged and tied to a chair, and on a table in front of her sat a laptop. She stared at me as if willing me to do something.

I bent down to get under the table and wiggled into the tight space beside her. "It's okay," I said as I untied the gag. They used Zip Ties to secure her feet and wrists. The confines of the cell didn't give her room to struggle. "Radim, do you have a knife?"

He checked his pocket and brought out a Swiss Army contraption. "It might not be enough," he said as he tossed it to me.

"I'll try not to hurt you more," I said.

"Just get me out of here," Rio said through cracked and swollen lips. "They promised to kill me when they got back."

"You won't be here." I maneuvered the small saw between the plastic and her wrist. I drew it back and forth a few times and the tie broke.

I released her ankle and she worked her fingers and flexed her foot. She'd been tied up long enough to lose feeling in both.

I couldn't reach around to the other side, so I backed out of the cell and repositioned myself. Her left side was tighter to the wall. I rolled under the table and cleared her ankle.

"Will you be able to climb out?" Radim asked Rio as I worked.

"Do I have a choice?" she asked, her voice gaining strength. "Nothing is broken, so probably, but I don't think I can run." She drew in a deep breath and then coughed on the exhale.

"How did they get you in here?" I asked.

The final tie around her left wrist was a problem. I couldn't get an angle on the saw that let me use it. I would have to poke at the lock until it gave.

There was some kind of screwdriver in the tool. I tried that but it didn't get in enough to make a difference. I pulled out all the pieces and found a pointy thing — not sure what it was for, but it would do for this. I had to hold it in my fingertips to get it in and my hands were pulsing with pain now. The angle meant I couldn't get enough force to break the lock but poking it would work.

"The table is new." Rio kicked the leg. "They tied me up out there and carried me in here."

"Why a computer?" Radim asked.

I appreciated his efforts to keep her mind off the time it was taking me to deal with the last restraint. My finger-tips screamed in pain at the effort of holding the tool firmly enough to poke the plastic lock. It only released a few clicks at a time. I knew it would be easier when I had a bigger gap, but I wasn't sure I could get there.

"They kept trying to get me to log into the university system. I told them it wouldn't work, but they just kept making me try."

"How are you getting a signal?" I asked. Only a few more pokes to go and I could let my fingers rest.

"The hole in the roof." Rio twisted her wrist as the tie became looser. "I think I can pull it out."

"Stop doing that. I can't get at the lock unless it's down and toward me," I said. I didn't want her getting another injury. I knew that she was close to the edge and even a little damage as she pulled out her hand might drain all her energy.

"We changed your password."

I felt the table shift and then jerk an inch away.

"I figured. And the table is jammed. I said I could get out."

"Now," I said.

Rio pulled her hand out. I saw her legs straighten and then disappear as she scrambled over the table to the entrance of her cell. I was trapped for a moment until Radim lifted her away. I slid out and pushed into a more or less erect position. There was blood in the fingertips of my gloves.

The light flicked on.

"They're coming back," Rio said.

The kidnappers had barely been gone long enough to get outside. "How long?"

"It's some kind of remote. It goes off just after they leave and comes on just before they get here."

I looked to Radim. "We can't hide outside. They'll find us right away."

He turned to look down the tunnel leading out of the cells. Now that the light was on, it was easy to see. "Go now, or they will know. Maybe they will guess."

I looked Rio over. "We might need to swim."

"Okay." She was trembling. "I'll do what I have to do."

I heard footsteps. "Shit. Time to go." I bent down and crawled into the space. Rio was behind me and Radim took up the rear. A few feet in, the ceiling rose and the light faded. I tested the ground in front of me before moving; it dropped off. I laid down and reached with my hands. My fingertips touched dirt.

"It's not far, but be careful," I whispered. Then I did my best somersault roll and landed on my ass. Things crunched under me and I was glad for the dark.

I backed off a little to give Rio room. We both retreated to let Radim into the small space.

"Can you make the light on your phone less bright?" he asked.

I turned it on and scrolled the brightness to low. It looked like we had found another set of cells. For prisoners who no one expected to survive? There were two small rooms and the rest of the area was clear. The wall held bolts for chains.

"No one would crawl through here," I said. "To keep people locked up, I mean."

"You think there's another entrance?" Rio wandered away to search for her own answer. I watched the painfully slow movements, the way she protected her arm and hugged her ribs. No one was ready for a race to the fresh air.

I heard shouting. "What are they saying?"

"They are scared," Radim said. "They found the trapdoor open when they got there."

I hadn't thought to close it, and even if I had, I'm not sure I would have willingly done it. "Do they know we're here?"

"One is looking down the passage." He held up his hand for silence so he could listen.

I looked around for Rio. She was at the edge of the glow from my phone. I glanced at the battery. It would be good for a while, but we weren't going to be making any more movies.

"Turn off the phone. Get in one of the cells." Radim grabbed Rio and pulled her into the dark hole across from me.

I heard a scrape of material in the tunnel and the little glow that came through went out. We were screwed if he came inside. I still had the Swiss Army knife; maybe I could drive the corkscrew into his eyeball. That is, if I could see him.

Light flooded the small room but didn't penetrate the cells. The brightness retreated and then died.

No one moved. I listened to the argument raging at the other end of the tunnel, frustrated that I was the only one who couldn't understand. The voices broke off.

I started counting seconds in my head. When I reached what I thought was three minutes and there were no sounds, I slid one foot in front of the other, trying to remember the distance between me and Radim and Rio. The openings to the cells had been across from each other, so if I held a straight course, I should eventually reach them.

I bumped into a soft body far too soon.

"One is gone," Radim whispered. "The other is waiting. The one who came through here didn't want to enter. He said too many sounds were coming from the tunnel at night."

"We need to let Jack know we have her," I said. "Get the police here."

"No," Rio hissed. "You can't trust anyone he sends. You don't know him. No one does except me. He made this happen."

Chapter 24

Suddenly too many things buzzed in my brain. We were trapped; maybe there was a way out behind us.

Should we risk jumping the one guy outside?

We could steal his weapon.

We could fight our way out if it came to that.

It was too dark to see the others.

Jack was involved. What the fuck did that mean? Dads aren't saints. I'm an adult, I know that. But would he really do this to his own child?

"What do you mean?" I clung to the newest revelation. "Your father wouldn't do this to you."

"I said you don't know him. You think he's some big shot lawyer. I know you think he's a pain in the ass too, but you have no clue."

I decided we needed light. If only one of the kidnappers stood on the other side of the tunnel, I could deal with him. I turned on the flashlight app and dimmed it a little more.

It helped. Being able to see even a little seemed to sort things out in my head. Rio stood next to Radim. She wrapped her arms around herself. I took off my jacket and handed it to her.

"I know Jack is a bit shady," I said. "But... what they did to you... I can't believe he knew all along."

"Something happened to him a couple of years ago. That's why I wanted to come here for university. I hoped if I got far enough away, he couldn't drag me into it."

"We need to move," Radim said. "We can sort the rest out when we are out."

Neither option seemed safe, or rather one didn't seem any less dangerous than the other. "Are you sure there is a way out? If we have to swim, I don't think Rio will make it." I figured we were deep enough underground we wouldn't need to jump far into the river. In fact, it smelled like the place flooded pretty regularly.

"He said they heard noises," Rio reminded me. "I'm not superstitious. I think it was people. If there's a door leading to the outside, sound would travel, right?"

"How could an exit that used to dump people into the river now empty into the street? Is there something you know about ancient Prague?" I believed that they would toss the bodies out, but maybe the river flowed closer in the past. Maybe the way out did lead to a busy street.

"I study data," Rio said. "My history is only just above the average tour guide."

I noticed her shiver despite being wrapped in my jacket.

"Only what I learned in school," Radim said. "It is not reliable."

Even I was getting frustrated with my inability to make a decision. Without information, I had to rely on my gut. "I think we go looking for this other exit," I said. "If it turns out to be a wash, we can still come back." And hope they hadn't brought in reinforcements while we were gone.

Radim moved to the entrance to the cell. He held up his hand and cocked an ear toward the tunnel. Then he stepped out of the weak light and disappeared into the dark behind us.

"Does he do that a lot?" Rio asked.

"You mean act like we're not here? Yes."

He came back and beckoned us to follow deeper.

My back ached from bending over, but I gritted my teeth and followed behind Rio. I had my handy corkscrew if anyone came up on us.

At the back of the room, Radim had found an exit. I could see where hinges would have been. Now they were clear of anything but some rust stains and a few clumps of rat hair at the bottom. I refrained from pointing it out.

"Let me explore first," Radim said. "If it is a trap or a dead end, it will be easier for one person to turn around."

If I was one of those tiny women, I would have volunteered to go first. But I wasn't and if Radim was willing to brave the possible rat den, I wouldn't stand in his way.

"How long do we wait?" Rio asked, her voice small.

"I promise we will do everything we can to get you out alive," he said. "I don't think the passage is long."

She was waning fast. I'm not sure I would have held up as well as she had if I believed my father had ordered someone to kidnap me and beat me up.

"We'll be fine," I said.

He nodded and slipped into the dark. He should have used his phone for light.

"Why do you think your dad is involved?" I wanted to know, and I knew talking would make the time pass faster.

"You saw the data I had?" She rubbed her arms for some heat.

"Yes, but we couldn't understand it," I said. "We had

someone look at it who might know, but she could only make out some aspects."

"Good. I want to be the one who makes it public knowledge." She looked down the passage, as if Radim was about to come out. "You know I'm smarter than most people my age, right?"

"As I understand it, you're smarter than most people of any age."

She sighed. "I guess. Well, it didn't help me make friends. When I was a kid, you know, when you make friends for the first time, I didn't know how to keep my mouth shut. No one wanted to play with me after a while because I was always correcting them."

"Sounds lonely," I said. She didn't need to know that most friends made at five years old didn't stay that way very long. In fact, most didn't stay with you until you reached the ripe old age of six. "So, you just studied?"

"Yes. I'm a cliché. But I liked it. Facts don't bully you or hurt your feelings. Now I'm here, it's kind of self-preservation. The other students party a lot. I really don't fit in."

All I could think to say were the platitudes I was sure she'd heard over and over. I got the feeling she didn't care that much anyway. Other people probably wouldn't change. She would.

"So, I decided to be the youngest PhD candidate at the university. What you saw in the files is two years of gathering, sorting, and analyzing financial transactions. I originally thought I'd do something on the lines of how money moved around the world in response to conflict."

"And now?"

"It didn't take long to realize it was a no-brainer and not worth doing. I guess I was more idealistic than I thought. Then I noticed relationships between the implementation of money laundering legislation and the direction of the transactions."

I heard shuffling footsteps. Radim was on his way back. "So you found patterns in criminal funds?"

"I looked at the history of the data and started a list of predictions. Who would be caught and whose money was confiscated. I thought I was just guessing."

"Then you checked," I said. "How accurate were you?"

"Ninety percent. And when I dug into the investigations where I was wrong, I found that I had just identified a higher-level criminal; the cops had taken down a low level one."

I needed time to think of a plan. We couldn't simply hand Rio over to Jack, but would she work with the RCMP? Or Interpol? She was in no shape to answer more questions.

"We can't go that way," Radim said, stepping into the room. "The exit is blocked."

I wanted to know who Rio had found that the authorities missed, but that could wait. "So we need to go through the other room."

"We can only do it one at a time," Radim said. "It could be a slaughter."

Chapter 25

In my head, I had a picture of us crawling on our bellies and sticking our heads out, ready to be killed one at a time. I'd forgotten how the tunnel actually allowed you to crouch before the opening. Radim went first as usual. I wasn't stupid enough to argue about it. He'd be no use in here if one of us were dead.

My thighs were burning three steps in. Radim came to a stop. We were too close to the exit to talk, so I had to trust he had a plan.

I could hear the one kidnapper talking. He must have been on the phone by the cadence of pauses. Once again, I was the only person in the dark about what was being said.

Radim's muscles tensed and then he was gone. I scurried forward and leapt into the room. The short wait gave me a chance to blink out the shock of the brightness. There was no one in there.

Rio followed me out and I pointed her to the nearest cell.

The kidnapper stepped out of her old one, yelling something.

Radim barreled into him and they both went down. The kidnapper had a gun, but his holster was under his body.

"Find something to tie him up," Radim grunted with the effort of holding the man and dodging the fist of his free hand.

I looked around, but there was nothing to use for restraints. The Zip Ties from Rio's cell were useless. I pulled off my tee-shirt and cut it with the Swiss Army scissors. It was taking too long. I tried to grip and tear it into strips, but between the blood and the sweat in my gloves, it kept slipping.

Rio shoved strips of her tee-shirt into my hands and then ran back into hiding.

I knelt beside the kidnapper who'd given up trying to punch Radim and was now tilting his hips to roll Radim off his body.

I flicked out the Swiss Army corkscrew and held it close to his face. He froze, his eyes focused on my hand.

"You speak English?"

"Yes."

Radim took the strips of fabric from me.

"You move, you lose an eye."

"I don't believe you," he risked a glance at my face. "You ever kill a man?"

"You don't want to find out," I said.

Radim rolled the kidnapper away from me, pulled his arms behind him and tied them. Then he removed the gun from the holster. "Get up." He gave a kick to the man's side to encourage him.

He struggled to his feet, listing a little to the right when he was standing.

"Now what are you going to do?" he asked. "Only one way out. My partner will be on his way back."

I levered myself off my knees and pushed him toward the cell. "Is he just as tough as you?"

"Tougher." He grinned, bloodstained teeth making him look like a maniac.

Rio joined us. "Why?" She looked him over and then kicked his knee. The man went down swearing. "I don't really care what the answer is. That was for beating me."

He wheezed. "The man who ordered us to take you is more frightening than this child."

"I guess you'll get to test that out in prison," I said. "Rio, wait outside."

"What are you going to do?" She edged closer, getting between Radim and the prisoner. "You don't need to protect me. I can look after myself."

I couldn't let her do any more damage. She was facing years of treatment for her trauma and if she lashed out now, she might do something that would never heal.

"You'll be safer out there." I hadn't thought ahead enough and had nothing planned for the prisoner, but maybe Radim had a way to make him talk that wouldn't cross the line. The problem was I knew the line became thin once you approached it.

"She won't leave," Radim said. "Unless you will go with her. We should all go anyway. I have the gun. We can send the police when we are in the hospital."

"If you shoot that down here, the report will burst our eardrums." I had fired a weapon a couple of times at a gun range in Richmond. I didn't like them, but I figured it was safer for me if I learned how to use one. "Last resort, right?"

"You can do more with a gun than fire it," Radim said. "We go?"

"You aren't going anywhere." The other kidnapper stood outside the cell. "Now we have more hostages. Maybe more money."

Our prisoner lunged at me. I punched forward to push him back, aiming for his neck, hoping to knock the wind out of him. I forgot the corkscrew that stuck out between my fingers. It went through his throat. I heard a hiss of escaping air, then blood oozed around the metal and his eyes lost focus.

He fell to the floor, pulling the Swiss Army knife with him.

A crash came from behind me. Radim and Rio struggled with the other kidnapper. The gun was across the room. The chair we'd originally thought to use as a club lay broken on the ground beside it.

I rushed toward them, bending to grab a leg of the chair, looking for a way to help without making it worse.

Radim's fist landed square on the kidnapper's nose. He didn't seem to feel it.

Rio aimed her foot between his legs, but he brushed it away, upending her.

"Stay down," I yelled as I stepped past her, holding the chair leg out like a sword.

Radim pulled the man out of the way just as I was about to impale him. The kidnapper was focused on me and didn't see Radim change position. His feet wide, Radim reach up and grabbed the man's head and twisted.

I heard a crack, and then two dead criminals lay on the floor.

For a second, I couldn't hear anything. My lungs gasped for air, but no sound reached my ears. I could see Rio and Radim breathing, but everything seemed as lifeless as the two men at our feet.

Noise came back in a rush. The rasp of our breath echoed around the room.

"This is bad," I said. "I don't know what the law is here, but we're going to have a hard time explaining all this."

Radim took off his jacket and handed it to me. "Don't worry. All I need to do is make a call. This will all be cleaned up. The police will only know what we tell them."

"You've done this kind of thing before?" Rio was staring at the bodies, trembling.

"We should get out of here," I said. "It's possible, no it's probable, they called for help when they found you gone."

"Your father," Radim said. "He should know you are safe."

I did up the zipper on his jacket, feeling a little lost in the size. "We need to contact him, Rio."

"No. He'll just send someone else." Rio looked up at me. "We should get fixed up then figure out how to deal with him."

"We don't have much time," I said. "I'm sure he's learned I didn't pick up the diamonds by now."

"What did I miss?" Radim asked. "Never mind. Give me a minute." He went into Rio's cell and found the signal. He made two phone calls and came back. "This will be gone in a couple of hours. I'll take the key back when we're finished."

"Aren't you afraid that you'll be in trouble for being late with it?" My brain was refusing to deal with bigger issues.

"I'm more afraid of leaving you two unsupervised," he said, laughing. "You both need to see a doctor. When we get out, a friend will be waiting to take you. Tell me why you won't call your father as we walk."

We didn't move as fast as we had coming in. Or, maybe

it just felt that way. Rio wasn't strong enough to talk and hurry, so I gave Radim the highlights of what Rio told me: Jack the bad guy, money laundering, all the shitty stuff she'd found out.

He paused and looked Rio over. "When you have been attended to, then you can tell me everything."

"What about the other people in on this? The second kidnapper went for help. They might come looking for us." Rio's voice was tight. Pain and fear can do that.

"Going to a doctor could bring the cops in," I said. "We can't let this become official."

"You are hurt," Radim said, ignoring me. "I have a friend who will help."

"Is anyone in this city not a friend?" I laughed, slightly hysterically.

"Some people still need to learn the value of my friendship."

Rio shivered beside me. It was cold but I worried about shock. "Okay, we do need medical help. But what about the kidnappers? Someone might be on the way."

"All they will find is that we are gone. They know Rio is hurt, but maybe they will think she'd rather hide than seek help."

We reached the steps out of the dungeon and Radim went ahead to make sure it was clear. I had no more fight in me. The idea that I would need to use my hands to help me climb to the top turned my stomach with anticipated pain. I slid them into the pockets of Radim's jacket so I wouldn't reach for the walls.

"It is safe," Radim called down.

I sent Rio up and followed two steps behind. The first breath of dry air was like sucking in life. Then I saw another man with Radim, and I tensed even though I knew he couldn't be a danger.

"This is Stefan. He will take you to a doctor. I will come as soon as I hand over the key to my other friends."

Stefan smiled and took Rio's arm. "It's okay, you come."

I followed Stefan to his car. He settled us and patted Rio's knee like a grandfather. "Don't worry. We go now."

Maybe it was better that he didn't speak much. Now that we were away from immediate danger, I found my eyes closing. I looked at Rio; she was already asleep.

THE DOCTOR WAS in a laser clinic. Stefan had passed Rio a broad-brimmed hat and waited while she adjusted it. He told me to keep my hands hidden, then we walked into a clean smelling reception area, all pale blue and gentle lights. The woman behind the counter was perfectly presented. She smiled as though we were on time for an appointment, rose and led us to a room in the back.

Stefan made sure we were comfortable and said goodbye.

The doctor cleaned and bandaged my hands first. Then he focused on Rio, inspecting her face gently and pronouncing her only bruised, not fractured. He promised it would heal without permanent damage and handed her a small pot of ointment.

"There is not much I can do to speed the healing," Doctor Ansel said. "It will be a week or more before you are back to normal. But you will get there."

Rio smeared balm on her cracked lips and thanked him.

"Anya will bring you food and water. I will leave some painkillers for you. Rest will be the best thing for both of you."

The door opened and Radim slipped inside, a plastic shopping bag in his hand. "Are you ready to go?"

"Wait," I said. "Your shoulder should be looked at. And we need to talk. Can we stay for a little while?" I thought of the promised food and drink.

Doctor Ansel passed me the bag and checked Radim.

"He will be fine if he rests the joint this time. You can stay as long as you want. Don't let him bully you." Doctor Ansel gave Radim a nod that seemed to carry more than an acknowledgment of the injury.

The bag contained two tee-shirts and a jacket.

"I hope they fit," Radim said. He turned his back while we changed. Everything was a size too big, but I didn't care how I looked.

Anya knocked while we were changing and handed us a six-pack of water and a bag of sandwiches. "Tell me when you are ready to go. I'll make sure no one is in the waiting room."

Then we were alone.

"Now you can tell us what you found," Radim said to Rio.

Chapter 26

"I think my dad was planning to make me work for him," Rio said.

Her words caught in her throat, and I wanted to let her rest, or at least give some context. But Radim had heard Jack enough, and I had told him plenty, that he couldn't think Rio meant working for the law firm.

She drank some water and then spoke, her voice little stronger. "When I was a kid, I would see people coming to the house. Dad would send me to my room, but he never checked to make sure I stayed there. I knew the people weren't clients, or not clients from the firm, anyway."

"How?" Radim asked.

"They talked about the wrong things. Enough clients came that I caught on to what they wanted to discuss, and I watched how they treated dad. Most of them were depending on him to help; they would be nice to me, and would listen to him. Some of them were scared of what might happen and would bluster, but always kept it businesslike."

"And the others?" I prompted her. We didn't have a lot of time before Jack would become suspicious.

"They were terrified of Dad. He would tell them what to do, and no one argued," she said. "So, I knew something was going on. I got into data analysis partly because I figured Dad wouldn't be able to use me in his other business."

"But he did find it valuable, yes?" Radim said. "This is not your fault. If you are right about him, he would find a way to exploit anything you did."

"We fought when I came here, but he agreed to pay. And then I dug up his secret." She squeezed the thin plastic bottle like a pump, staring at the water level as though she was testing the pressure. "He runs the money laundering for most of the big criminals in the world. Some you know, but there are lots you don't. Not only crime; he helps terrorists, and he doesn't care what they do with it. There's more, but I need to find the proof. I was close," she finally said. "It took me almost a year, but I found the links to him. I can prove what he's done. That was what changed him. Even before, when I knew he was shady, I felt loved. Suddenly I felt owned."

"Laszlo wasn't playing with us," I said. I turned to Radim. "Do you think he told Jack anything?"

"Laszlo was in too much of a hurry to hide," Radim said. "He wants to survive. Putting Jack away won't stop crime."

"Not all crimes, but his might stop, or slow down for a while," Rio said. "I can move the money somewhere else."

That would send killers after her. "Too risky. Now that they know what you can do, I don't think they will ignore anything," I said. "It won't be kidnapping next time."

She looked up from the water bottle. "Are you saying

we shouldn't do anything? I want to call the police. My dad needs to be stopped. I don't care about who takes over."

"I'm not saying that." I reached over and touched her shoulder. "We need to be smart about how we act."

I checked my phone. Jack had been sending texts for the last twenty minutes. "I guess he knows we didn't pick up the ransom," I said. "We need to make some decisions soon. If he ordered the kidnapping, he'll find out you are free before too much time passes."

"What decisions?" Rio asked. "I'm not backing down."

She may be brilliant, but Rio was still young. "This is not an all-or-nothing decision. Yes, he's going to prison, but you won't be safe if we just call the cops."

"I didn't think of that," Rio said. "It's stupid, but he's still my dad. I guess I still expect him to act like one. How do we do this so we're all protected?"

I looked at Radim, but he just nodded for me to continue. "First, they'll take everything your dad owns away."

"I can support myself." She must have seen the look on my face because she grinned and added, "I received five job offers in the last six months. None of them linked to my dad. I did a few consulting gigs. I earn enough of my own money to finish my PhD."

That made what we planned a little easier to live with. "We just need to make sure you receive a new identity," I said. "I hate to sound selfish, but I need him to pay me."

"You need to disappear too," Radim said. "I think it would be better if I helped with that. If the police can't find you, you don't need to get any deeper than you want to be."

"We'll worry about that after. Rio? Are you ready for what's coming? The police will want to put you in protective custody," I said. "You'll need to testify."

"Maybe when it's all over, Radim can find me a new life too?"

I couldn't see her letting go of her life so easily. The PhD could be done while she was waiting for the trial and then she'd have to let it go. That was a lot of work to toss away for a life of hiding. Also, someone as smart as Rio didn't blend in and there was no way she could hide her brilliance. "Maybe," I said. I looked at Radim again, hoping he would give some kind of hint that it could be done, but he looked away.

"So, we don't call the police until you get your money?" Rio asked. "If I can access a computer, I can deal with that right now."

Maybe the diamonds were still waiting to be picked up. Radim probably knew a fence. But I wanted more than just a paycheck. "I think I want Jack to pay me, thanks."

"He won't," she said. "And I won't be able to hide what I do once the cops take his assets."

"We'll use it," I said. "I think what we need to do is keep him on the phone long enough for the police to arrive. We need to know where he is when we're talking."

"Can we get out of here?" Rio asked. "I need a shower. I need something clean to wear after it. This is already starting to smell of sweat and blood."

"My place," Radim said. "My computer is there. You can clean up, but I have no clothes for you."

"My hotel," I said. "Rio can use a pair of my jeans and a tee-shirt." They would be too big, but at least they wouldn't be covered in sweat and blood.

"I would rather go home," Rio said.

I didn't want to say why that was a bad idea. "My hotel is better. There are some stores along the way if you don't want my things."

"We can argue all day," Radim said. "Sharka's room is

closer. We are probably a little safer there than anywhere because someone is always around."

Rio looked like she wanted to push for going home, but her shoulders slumped. "Fine."

Radim left us to check the waiting room.

I wasn't convinced she would stay with us when we left the doctor. "Your place is trashed," I said. It was the only way I could think to stop her from going home. "Sorry."

"It's okay." Rio stood and reached for her hat. "I'll have to find a new place anyway."

"The reception area is clear," Radim said.

Anya was absent as we hurried through the waiting room and out to the street. The noise of cars and people made me want to retreat back to the tiny room. We'd been through hell, but it had been quiet in the office at least.

We stopped at a department store. Radim paid for Rio's new outfit and then we walked the few blocks to my hotel.

"We can start while you shower," I said. "Unless you changed your mind about your dad?"

"So, the plan is to get your fee, and then delay him until the police arrive?" The way she said the words made me feel like she had no confidence in our success. "Sure. I just want it over. And really, he is my dad. If he's in custody, he might be safe. I'm not stupid enough to think those people who were scared of him won't retaliate."

She grabbed the clothes and went into the bathroom.

I HELD my breath as I sent a text to Michael. *Where is Jack right now?*

This was the worst part of being nine hours different and a world away. I couldn't walk into Jack's office and hold him there.

Most plans went wrong somewhere because you couldn't predict everything. This plan was so full of unknowns that I hesitated to call it a plan at all.

"You are sure this man will answer?" Radim asked.

I'd given him the number of an RCMP officer who owed me a favor, not that this was about paying me off. If it went even half well, he'd be up for a promotion and that would buy me some leeway if they decided I shouldn't disappear. "Give me a second."

I sent a text to Etienne. *Call coming from a number in Czech Republic. Don't ignore.*

He immediately replied with the smiling emoji.

Rio was sitting on the bed, Radim leaning against the short partition beside the desk. I was positioned so Jack wouldn't be able to see anything other than my face and the wall behind. I wanted to watch the results of our plan, and for that we needed more than a phone call.

In his office, Michael answered.

Keep him there.

"Ready?" I looked at Radim.

He had to be the one to make the call. I needed to be available to talk to Jack, and if the RCMP wanted to keep someone on the line, Radim was the right guy.

Radim dialed Etienne's number and put the phone on speaker.

"What is so important?" His voice was still that warm tone with a cute Quebec accent. That had been one of the reasons I ended up in his bed.

"You want the top money launderer in the country?" I asked.

"Always. You are not here?"

"On vacation," I said. He didn't need to be involved when I disappeared.

"What do you have for me?"

"Jack Hennessey," I said. "Is he on your radar at all?"

"Not high, but we know he is defending some of our biggest suspects. Should we bump him up?"

I told him about Rio's kidnapping and what she found. "I put a document in our favorite cloud with all the details." Then I had Rio explain how everything linked back to Jack.

"Your father is very good at hiding his real work," Etienne said. "Will you be willing to testify?"

"He had me kidnapped, beaten, and I'm pretty sure I'd be dead if he had my files."

"What about your research?" Etienne asked. "Will we need a warrant?"

"I'll give you what you need," Rio said. "Just make sure I can earn my PhD before my research is part of the court records, okay? I mean, they might decide I can't publish when the case is over. Or, maybe not at all."

"I cannot guarantee anything, but I will ask," Etienne said.

"How long before you can pick Jack up?" I hoped he had what he needed to get going, but nothing Rio was willing to share would be worth it if Jack got away.

"Is he expecting us?"

"We don't think so," I said. "He's in his office. I haven't called him, yet. I need to know how long you want me to stall."

"I need a half hour," Etienne said. "Can you hold him that long?"

"Yes," I said, not knowing if I was lying or being optimistic. "I don't have a choice, right?"

"And your accomplices in this escapade? Will they testify?"

Radim frowned at me.

"I did it all alone," I said.

"Hmm. It might be believed," Etienne said. "We will worry about that later. Keep him in his office. I will be there with my team."

We disconnected.

Chapter 27

"Keeping him talking that long is going to be impossible," Radim said. "He'll suspect something is wrong."

"We don't need to call until Michael says Jack's moving, right? I figure between Rio and me, we can keep him distracted for ten minutes. If it's a problem, Michael will come up with a stalling tactic."

We waited fifteen minutes before calling; I couldn't stand the delay any longer. In that time Jack sent me twenty texts that I left unanswered.

"Let's get proof," I said, turning to Rio. She sat a little straighter on the bed. She rubbed balm on her lips again and gave me as big a smile as she could manage. I took her picture and sent it to Jack.

Where are you?

Skype.

My computer played the Skype song, announcing an incoming call. I set my phone to record and placed it out of his line of sight.

"Where are you? How is she? Let me talk to her."

Jack was trying really hard to seem like he cared.

Knowing the truth helped me stay focused on our plan. Stalling meant time to talk, not accuse.

"She's safe. I need my money."

I wanted to see Jack in handcuffs. Etienne's job was catching high-level criminals. He admitted that Jack was already on their radar. His bosses wouldn't delay in giving him his warrant. Since we'd received no warning about a problem, I only needed to keep going until Etienne marched in and arrested Jack.

"I want to talk to her," Jack said. His act was slipping, his eyes narrowing in suspicion. "It looks like you're at your hotel. Is she with you?"

"I moved hotels, Jack. Pay me and I'll tell you where you can pick up your daughter."

He leaned into the screen and I couldn't help but draw back. Knowing he couldn't actually grab me didn't stop my instincts from protecting me.

I glanced at the recording on my phone. It had only been two minutes. How was I going to keep this up?

"I'm not paying you until I have Rio," he said slowly and calmly.

"How do I know you'll pay me then?" I asked. I was running a script in my head, reminding myself that he couldn't touch me. He couldn't be sure whether I'd lied about the hotel. And that at any moment now he would be in cuffs.

He relaxed back in his chair. "You don't trust me? Why should I trust you?"

Radim shifted and I looked up. He shook his head. What did he mean? No one was coming to take Jack? I shouldn't trust him? The RCMP were waiting outside Jack's door?

"Who's there with you?"

That was a stupid mistake.

We'd managed to waste five minutes, but what if Etienne got delayed? What if he'd been too optimistic about the time? I wished I could ask Radim what he'd meant.

"No one. I was checking the time," I lied.

"Are you in a hurry?" Jack asked.

"To get paid and hand over your daughter," I said. "Why are you negotiating with me? I'm not asking for a ransom. I saved you ten million dollars and all I want is the rest of my money."

"If you don't tell me where she is, I'll tell the wrong people about your secret."

"You're bluffing. It will hurt you as much as me."

Now we were past the time I expected Etienne to burst through the door.

"What about Michael? His visa is up for renewal."

I'd been so concerned with Rio, I gave no thought to Michael being in danger. I risked a glance at Radim again and he was shaking his head. "Michael can take care of himself."

"What about Rio's research?" Jack asked.

"What about it? You wanted me to find your daughter." I silently thanked him for giving us another topic to argue over.

"You must have figured out what it was," Jack said. "I want to pass it along to the authorities. Send me that and I'll pay you. Then you can tell me where to find Rio."

I looked down at my swollen hands, stalling. The files couldn't be sent from the university. Unless Rio could do it. But Jack really only wanted that, not his daughter. Rio's life would be on a timer as soon as Jack had his proof. Mine too, I guess.

"I can get to the data," I said. "But you pay me now, or

I send it to the authorities myself." I saw his lips tighten. "I know you want the glory, Jack. Pay me and I'll step back."

"Did you hear? You murdered a woman before you left Vancouver?" Jack asked. "The police are looking for the final few clues before they issue an arrest warrant."

"You framed me?" I couldn't keep the surprise from my voice.

"Yes, and I did a great job. You'll never prove it's not real."

I couldn't just let it go. Jack had to think he was still in control. It was a struggle to make me sound like I was beaten rather than I didn't care. "Fine, they have to find me first."

"Doesn't anything but money grab your attention?" Jack asked.

"I didn't kill anyone," I said. "There will be a way to prove that. Why are you so determined to hang on to the money? If you could put ten million together that fast, my fee is nothing. Just pay me. You get your daughter and she can give you the research."

"I don't have time for this," Jack said. "Do you want it in the same account?"

He changed his mind too quickly, but I couldn't guess what he might have in the works to screw me. "Yes."

I heard a keyboard clicking. Then my phone pinged.

The money was in the account. I set the script in motion to hide the funds and waited until the account was empty before looking up.

I had nothing left to hold him.

I beckoned Rio from the bed.

"Daddy?" She did a good job of playing the distressed child.

"Rio, you're safe. Good. You must send me your

research. It's the only way to make sure this doesn't happen again."

I felt her tremble. Her fists were clenched. This wasn't fear. She had a temper like her dad. If she lost it, we wouldn't be able to watch him be arrested because he'd catch on to our plan. I touched her knee and she opened her hands.

"It will take a bit to get the university to release it. You remember how you insisted that my stuff should be held behind tight firewalls?"

So, Jack had been preparing for today since Rio came here. Maybe preparing wasn't the right word. I had to hope he'd tried to protect her at the beginning.

"Just send it," Jack said, his voice hardening again. "I don't want anything else to happen to you."

"Dad, that sounds like you're threatening me." She leaned in close. "You know what I found, right?"

That wasn't the script at all. I tried to pull her away from the screen, scrambling to make something up that would mitigate what she'd done. Where was Etienne?

"You are smarter than I expected," Jack said.

I noticed the door to his office crack open. Rio kept her eyes locked with Jack's.

"Why did you let them do this to me?" She pointed at her face. "Or was it your orders? How could you hurt me like this?"

"You wouldn't stop looking. You should know better than to keep digging into my business."

"I wasn't," Rio said. "I was just doing interesting research. I got that you were involved, but I only knew how deep when I heard my kidnappers talking."

"Next time I'll hire smarter criminals," Jack said. He pushed himself up from the desk. "You send me your proof, or I'll make sure you don't get another chance. I will find you no matter how hard you try to hide. I'm connected everywhere. I have dirt on so many people I don't need to go too far to find someone willing to kill to get me off their back."

Jack was so angry he didn't notice Etienne standing behind him. I saw other RCMP members in the doorway. I let a smile cross my lips.

"Jack Hennessey, you are under arrest for the kidnapping of Rio Hennessey and money laundering. I'm sure we'll find a few more charges when we have you in custody."

Jack tried to resist, but Etienne cuffed him and handed him off to another member of the force.

"See you when you come home, Sharka. I look forward to hearing the whole story." He ended the call.

"Is it over?" Rio asked.

Her knees buckled and I caught her before Radim had a chance. "The hard part," I said. "Well, the dangerous part. It's going to be difficult giving testimony against your dad no matter what he did."

"Not hard at all. He just threatened to do this all over again." Rio shook out the tension in her body. "How soon can we get back there to make statements?"

"We'll take the next flight," I said.

Radim raised an eyebrow at me.

"I know I said I wouldn't go back, but I don't think I have a choice."

Chapter 28

It took a month. I met with lawyers and RCMP officials every day, or that's what it seemed like. Rio was checked over by a doctor as soon as we passed customs. She spent twenty-four hours in the hospital; they wanted every test possible done on her so the defense wouldn't be able to undermine her testimony by pointing out her injuries and implying brain damage.

Jack's threat about framing me for murder was just a bluff, although I didn't doubt he would have followed through if not for the arrest.

The RCMP analysts dove into Rio's research for other names. She was helping them and thriving in their environment when she wasn't writing her PhD thesis.

In that month, I found a way to say goodbye to all the people I originally planned to abandon. Etienne was the hardest. I felt like I'd dumped all the problems in his lap and then decided to walk away. He refused to let me sink into self-pity — his words. I was just grateful they didn't need my testimony in court.

Radim confirmed he had a new identity for me when I called him.

Michael had sent me a text while Rio and I flew back. Now that the RCMP were there, it was too dangerous for him to stick around. He promised to send me his new contact information. I hoped he didn't change his mind.

When the money Jack paid me was hidden, I paid half my fee to Radim despite his protests that I just owed a favor. I didn't want that debt.

Now I was walking out of the Prague airport again; this time off a one-way ticket and no messages from home.

"Welcome back," Radim said. "You need a ride?"

I laughed. This was so different from my last trip; no exhaustion, a first-class flight that let me sleep when I needed to, and jet lag wouldn't be a problem.

"So, they let you leave?" He led me to a black Mercedes.

I tossed my bags in the trunk and joined him. "I didn't do anything wrong." I still carried the secret of that beating. There was no one who could talk now, and I could do some good to try to make up for my mistake.

"And Jack? He won't send his friends after you?"

News is global now, but I guess this wasn't interesting enough for the big agencies. "Jack got shanked in jail. Someone killed him before they could process the charges."

"Do you think someone ordered it?"

"No idea. Jack wasn't the kind of guy to just get along. It could have been something he did on his first day. Or it could have been one of the people he thought he could blackmail." I couldn't raise enough emotion to decide which option I wanted. "That kind of thing is tricky. As likely to get you silenced as it is to get you power."

"So, our first adventure ends?"

"Rio has leads on other members of the conspiracy. The money they know about was confiscated." I remembered Laszlo's words. "There's going to be chaos for a while. But I'm done. They don't have a clue about you, so as far as I can tell, the answer is yes."

Radim turned away from the city.

"What about Lazlo?" I asked.

"Did he order the killing?" Radim asked. He kept his eyes on the road and I couldn't tell if that was because he didn't want me to see the truth in his eyes.

"I meant was he back in Prague. But now you ask, do you think he would do it?"

"Yes," Radim said. "And you do too. I don't know if he did."

"Where are we going?" I didn't have any immediate plans, other than improving my Czech and resting.

"You still want a country house?"

"Yes. More than ever actually."

I'd done some research in the last few weeks, along with language lessons, something I should have done before I came a month ago. "I know all the restrictions, and the paperwork, and how to set up as a business."

"I have a friend." He laughed at my expression. "Yes, I always have a friend. This one wants to sell his family home and move to Vienna. I thought you should meet."

I relaxed back into the leather seat. "You are determined to put me in your debt for a favor."

"It is the way we work," he said. "I might need a place for someone to hide out for a while. Only little crimes, I promise."

I didn't care what size the crimes were. Today I felt like I'd been waiting all my life to take control of my fate. Working with Radim's friends had benefited me so far. I trusted him to keep it that way.

Want More?

Want more gritty mysteries with determined female investigators? Use the QR code to check out the first book of The Charity Deacon Investigation, HUBRIS.

Sneak peek on the next page.

If you enjoyed reading In The Shadow of the Past, please consider helping other readers to find the story by leaving a review.

Chapter 1

I'm a P.I. I know that sounds cool and dangerous, but mostly it's just seedy. Every now and then I feel like chucking it all in, but then someone asks for my help, and I get back in the groove. When I'm in the groove, I follow wandering spouses, dig into employees' finances, and occasionally track down a missing person.

When I'm not doing the PI thing, I do a little journalism. I've also waited tables, driven a tour bus, and put in a few shifts at a retail store. That's me, Charity Deacon, five foot eight inches of black haired, blue eyed, Renaissance woman.

I was sitting on the patio of the Starbucks on the corner of Robson and Thurlow. It was fall and the pumpkin lattes were in season. Just as I started to zone out, a screeching crash broke the mood.

The noise came from a white Jeep bouncing off the back of a bus across Thurlow. I dropped my latte and grabbed my camera, clicking pictures as I ran.

Sirens wailed closer.

I could see that the bus was empty. Out of the corner

of my eye, I saw the driver running from the Starbucks across the intersection – yes there are two – carrying a coffee in one hand, and pulling his mobile phone out of his pocket with the other. He threw the coffee in the middle of the street when it got in the way of dialing.

As I reached the Jeep, a police car pulled up. One of the cops jumped out and ran to yank open the driver's door. A body fell sideways and hung from the seatbelt. I could tell it was a body, and no longer a person, because it flopped and there was white powder from the airbag all over its face. The powder stained red from the blood oozing from the hole just below his ear.

I took pictures then ran around to the other side before the police could stop me. The passenger door opened, and a man stumbled out before folding at the knees, and planting his face on the asphalt. I kept snapping for a dozen more shots and then focused on the street action.

"Miss, please step back." One of the cops walked into my camera range, a blurry flesh colored barrier between the action and me.

I obeyed. Well, technically the small step I took was back. Switching to video mode, I started panning the crowd. The cop put his hand in front of the lens.

"Step farther back," he said.

I tried not to sigh. I knew from my history with the cops, it would just antagonize him. "I'm not in the way. I'm not interfering. What's the problem?"

"Can I get your name and address, please?"

"Why?"

"You were a witness." The cop looked at my camera. It felt like a threat. Maybe that was because I'd been threatened by the cops before. They didn't like it when people pointed out their failings.

I reminded myself to keep my tone even. "That doesn't mean I can't take pictures."

The cop sighed. "Look, you can give me your details now, and I'll let you take the pictures while we get the other statements. Or, you can wait over there until we get around to taking your statement and you lose your photo op. Your choice."

"Fine. Charity Deacon, number 9 Dock B, 1525 Coal Harbour Quay, 604 555 5555."

He wrote it down, and then I went back to videoing the bystanders.

"Don't go anywhere without giving us your statement."

I ignored him and swept my camera over the gathering crowd, recording the cop's head as he walked across my line of sight. "Asshole," I muttered.

I shot a video of the people on the sidewalk, mostly people trying to see and not see at the same time. Turning, I scanned across the street. A few cars were backed up at the intersection, but one in particular caught my attention. Two men stood beside a black SUV, both well dressed and well built. What made them stand out were the smiles they wore; identical and smug.

I swung the camera past to get a panorama before checking the battery level, almost out. I flicked back to photo and snapped pictures of as many people as I could. The two men climbed back into their vehicle and drove away as I took the last few shots.

When I got back to the Starbucks patio, the bus driver was talking to one of the constables. "I'll get fired for this," he moaned. "I'm not supposed to stop there."

"Look at it this way," the cop answered. "If the bus wasn't there to stop the Jeep, we'd be carting a few more bodies to the morgue, and a lot more to the ER."

I made a mental note to call Transit and commend the

actions of the bus driver. The cop was right, and the guy shouldn't get shit for taking a quick break.

There were three other uniformed cops taking statements from the twenty or so people who had stopped to see what was going on.

While I waited, I had some time so I tried to add a little to my bottom line with my photos. I made some calls, the Vancouver Sun and Province, the Courier, and the local TV news station. The newspapers told me they would take my pictures if I could send the files by the evening deadline, but the TV station already got their footage from someone else.

Chapter 2

That same afternoon, my best friend Lu and I sat on the rooftop patio of my floating home in Coal Harbour, enjoying a bottle of Malbec and a plate of nibbles.

The marina was quiet. Most of the boats that surrounded our small community of houses were docked and deserted. There were a few seagulls circling for scraps, but they weren't screaming.

I liked the contrast between the peace of the marina, and the bustle of the community outside the gate.

Lu and I had been friends since the first day of kindergarten when I'd run onto the playground at recess looking forward to playing. Instead of the swings my eyes focused on four of the biggest kids surrounding this tiny Asian girl who was standing with her fists clenched and face red, clearly trying not to cry. I stomped over, shoved two of the bullies out of my way, and stood next to her with my fists raised.

Since then, we've stood side by side through every important event: her wedding, and then her husband's funeral five years later, my first real relationship, from passionate start to disastrous end, and my parent's memorial service.

She played with the four heavy gold bands circling her wrist. "If you think those men were up to something, why didn't you call the cops and tell them what you saw?"

"I didn't know it was anything." I held up the bottle, but Lu shook her head, so I poured the remainder into my glass. "I mean, it looked suspicious, but maybe they were just checking to see if there was anything they could do?"

"You don't sound like you believe that." Lu raised an eyebrow. "You said they looked proud."

I hate it when she's got a point. "You know, the cops don't like me right now. What would I have said to them anyway?"

Lu twitched her mouth in a smile. "How about something like, I think those two men might have had something to do with this. Charity, your job isn't to prove anything. It's to point out something you think might be important."

I had hoped for some encouragement, but Lu was right. I should probably have told the cops, even though some of them are still pretty ticked at me. It's not my fault one of their own was beating his wife, and I found out. Although, I guess they might have reason to blame me for going to the press. "Well, actually, my job is to investigate cases for my clients."

"True." Lu checked her watch. "You keep telling me that, but you also keep telling me you are tired of investigating people's problems. If you don't commit to this, you'll never get better at it."

I couldn't argue with that. "I know, I know. I just feel like I need to do more important stuff than taking pictures of cheating spouses."

She laughed and flicked at a mosquito. "Then you need to get better at it, so you can get better cases."

"Yeah, we can talk about that later. Right now, I'm making enough money to do what I need, so let's leave it."

"But I know you've forgone the pay part of it a couple of times."

"I can afford to do some pro bono work." I thought that sounded much more professional than free. "It's only when I think the job will be easy."

"I know, but you aren't always right." Lu swallowed the last drop of wine in her glass. "I've given up trying to talk you out of that stuff. I was just making an observation. In fact, what does Mike think about your adventures in pro bono?"

Mike was my uncle, and my only living relative. I hadn't mentioned today's events to him, yet. "Nothing. He helps me with connections, but he doesn't feel the need to comment."

"Sure." Lu laughed. "It must be helpful to have connections in the – what? Spy world? Oh yeah, he's a security consultant. Speaking of connections, send me some pictures, and I will see if I can get anything for you."

"I thought it was too dangerous."

"It is but I'll be discreet."

"Well, I'll check the pictures and video more carefully tonight," I said. "I'll talk to the cops tomorrow if I can find anything more than just suspicion."

"Good." Lu looked over at my neighbor's roof. "Is Jake still working on that series about the mayor?"

Before I could answer, I heard the doorbell ring, then a rapid knocking, and a "hey are you home?"

"Shit, that's all I need. You know Delores is going to tear me a new one for the noise." I ran through the bedroom and downstairs.

I pulled the door open to see a skinny Asian girl dressed in a black miniskirt, torn fishnet stockings, cropped tee shirt, and piercings in lips, eyebrow, and nose.

"Jeez, how did you get through the security gate?" I looked down toward Delores Markham's house. Relieved that no one was peering through the curtains. "Who are you? What do you want?"

"Nice way to welcome a client, bitch." The girl looked like a child and carried herself like a biker. "An old guy let me in."

Most of my neighbors were pretty careful about the security gate. "Did he know he let you in?"

"Maybe not." The girl shrugged. "You going to let me in? I got a job for you."

I checked her out and decided that between Lu and I, we were probably safe from any trouble this kid could cause. I stepped aside to let her into the living room. "What's your name?"

"Val."

"Val what?"

"Just Val."

"How did you know where I lived?" I saw Lu peek around the corner of the stairs and nodded her to stay up there.

"A guy told me." Val looked around the small room. I hoped she wasn't casing the joint. "So, you ask all your clients this many questions?"

"I usually don't meet people in my home." I kept my client meetings at coffee shops. It was easier than trying to dodge impatient ones on the wharf. "Would you like a soda?"

"A beer would be better."

"I'm pretty sure you aren't old enough." I passed Val a diet Coke and pointed to the dining area. Pulling out a pad of paper from the backpack I'd left hanging on the back of my chair, I asked, "How old are you anyway?"

"I'm eighteen."

I raised an eyebrow.

"Okay, I'm sixteen. You find people, right?" She turned the can around clicking her black painted nails on the side.

"I take missing persons cases, yes. Who's missing?" I couldn't figure out why she was being so aggressive when she wanted me to help.

"The guy said you were good." Val continued to play with the can. Looking closer, I could see a bruise under the thick makeup on her face. I saw another, older bruise showing on her arm.

No needle marks, which I took as a good sign.

"Where do you live?"

She didn't answer.

"Can you tell me where you live?" This was getting tired. If she didn't start answering questions, I wouldn't be able to help her.

"Why, you got some kind of residency requirement?" Val started to bounce on the ball of her right foot as though she was getting ready to run. The movement caused her entire body to shake, but she seemed oblivious to it.

I put my pen down and took the can from Val. "Look, you came to me. You banged on my door like the devil was after you. Tell me what you want or get out. I have things to do."

"Okay, chill. I need to know how much it will cost." She reached into her pocket and pulled out a wad of bills. "I can put this down now and get you more later… when you find her."

"Where did you get the money from?" I thought I knew what Val was going to say.

"You think my money is dirty? Look, I earned this." She pushed the bills toward me. "I didn't steal it."

I ignored the money. "Tell me who's missing."

Val forced her lips together and swallowed before speaking. "My sister, she disappeared."

The shell was cracking, and I saw the scared child inside. "Where are your parents?"

"Turning to worm food." Val's casual shrug didn't match with the catch in her voice. "It's only Emma and me."

"I'm sorry." I remembered how alone I'd felt when my parents had died in India. That was the hardest call I had ever had to take. "What did the police say?"

"Hah. You think the cops are interested in looking for a hooker. They got Picton and now it's like they think no other hookers count."

Despite the bravado, I could hear pain in the tightness of her voice. "That's not true and I think you know it. Did you go to the police?"

"No." Val looked down at her lap. "I don't want to get them involved."

Lots of my clients don't want the police involved. But, this time, that wouldn't work. I needed them to start a missing person's file. "Fine, where are you living?"

"I got a place, don't worry. What about my sister?"

Okay, I was done with this dancing around. If I couldn't get an answer to my questions, I'd see if she could do as I asked. "I don't like taking a case that should be with the police. I need you to go report her missing. Come back with a case number, and I'll think about it."

Val stopped bouncing her foot and looked up. "Only think about it?"

"That's all I'll promise." I wasn't sure I wanted to get

involved, but I didn't want to say no now that she'd pulled in her thorns.

"Okay." Val sighed. "I'll do it now and come right back."

"No. Just phone, give me the case number, and tell me what the police say." I needed to get back to those pictures and I hoped the cops would solve her problem.

"Fine. If you don't want to help me, you should just say so." Val stared at the money on the table. "Is it because of the money? It's not dirty, you know."

"It's not the money." I felt sorry for her. The thorns were back out, but she seemed to be wearing an armor made of attitude, one I'd seen on a lot of street kids. She was still a kid, and by the way she swallowed before talking about her sister, a scared kid. "Look. I think the police will investigate, but give me some information now, and I'll see what I can find out. What's her name?"

"Emma."

I almost told her to forget it. If I was going to have to drag every bit of information out of her, it was going to be an uphill battle. But she was so young under that attitude, I couldn't do it. "I need a last name. I can't find someone by just a first name."

"Wei. Our last name is Wei."

"That wasn't so hard, was it? When did she disappear?"

"The last time I saw her was two days ago. She was going out to start work."

"What does she do?"

"She's a hooker. So what?" Her eyes shone, chin jutted.

"Val, I need to know where to start looking."

"Oh, okay. She works down on the Eastside, and some-times around The Drive."

"What does she look like? Do you have a picture?"

"No. No pictures. She's a bit taller than me."

Val was at least four inches shorter than me. "So, five five, or six?"

"Uh huh. Her hair has red streaks in it, and it's cut short and spiky."

"Okay, any tats or piercings?"

"Yep. A butterfly on her ass."

Was she trying to be deliberately obstructive? "Val, stop fighting me on this. If you can't just answer my questions, I can't help you. Now, anything I might see when she has her clothes on?" I heard the annoyance snap in my voice. *Calm and professional.*

Val shook her head. "She tried to look straight. We were going to get off the street. She didn't want to mark herself as a hooker."

"What was she wearing the last time you saw her?" I kept scratching notes on the pad, trying not to look at Val, trying not to antagonize her.

"Jeans, a white wife beater and red stilettos."

"Who is her pimp?"

"No pimp. We look after each other."

"Okay." I flipped the pages back and pulled out a business card. "You go talk to the cops, and call me at this number when you're done."

Val looked at the card, turned it over and back. "Charity Deacon Investigations. Sounds very official." She sniffed.

"It is." I stood and pointed to the door. "The sooner you get to the police station, the better."

"Fine, I can take a hint." Val jerked up from the chair. "I'll call you as soon as I'm done with the cops."

I escorted her to the security gate and pulled it tight when she walked away. Val burst out laughing then strode off.

Lu was watching from the patio when I ran back to the house. "Hey, I thought you were focusing on the case from this afternoon."

"Hush, the neighbors don't need to know everything that's going on." I shut the door and grabbed a bottle of white wine from the fridge before going upstairs.

Lu pushed her glass toward me. "I heard everything. What are you going to do?"

"Hope the police will take the case seriously." I didn't think they would do much but hoping doesn't take any effort.

Lu shook her head. "I'm sure they will, but taking it seriously, and finding a missing person isn't the same thing."

"Well, I'll ask around a bit and help her out. It can't hurt." I poured wine into our glasses.

Lu picked up hers and I heard her mutter, "I'm sure it can," before taking a sip.

IF YOU WANT MORE, use the QR code to check out HUBRIS.

Free book

Claim your copy of Buying Into Death when you sign up for my newsletter and follow Charity as she solves her fastest case yet!

Also by P A Wilson

For more books by P A Wilson

Use the QR code below or go to pawilson.ca

About the Author

Perry Wilson is a Canadian author based in Vancouver, BC who has big ideas and an itch to tell stories. Having spent some time on university, a career, and life in general, she returned to writing in 2008 and hasn't looked back since (well, maybe a little, but only while parallel parking).

She is a member of the Vancouver Writers Social Group, The Royal City Literary Arts Society, and The Surrey Writing Workshop. Perry has self-published several novels. She writes the Madeline Journeys, a fantasy series about a high-powered lawyer who finds herself trapped in a magical world, the Quinn Larson Quests, which follows the adventures of a wizard named Quinn who must contend with volatile fae in the heart of Vancouver, and the Charity Deacon Investigations, a mystery thriller series about a private eye who tends to fall into serious trouble with her cases, and The Riverton Romances, a series based in a small town in Oregon, one of her favorite states. Her stand-alone novels are Breaking the Bonds, Closing the Circle, and The Dragon at The Edge of The Map.

For more information
www.pawilson.ca
pawilson@pawilson.ca

f X

Acknowledgments

People think that the process of writing is solitary. That's not the case for me. I have help from so many people it would be hard to acknowledge everyone, but I'll give it a try.

The support and inspiration I get from my writer's groups is incalculable. The Vancouver Writers Social Group opens my mind to other ways of telling a story. The Royal City Literary Arts Society gives me the opportunity to meet and share with other writers who have more knowledge than I do. The Other 11 Months group is where I learn about getting the words on the page. And my critique group who helps me find the best parts of the story I want to tell. Thanks to all of the members of these great groups.

Last of all, but definitely a huge part of the process, my beta readers. These are the people who love stories and are willing, and more than able, to tell me if my finished story is ready for you, my readers.

www.ingramcontent.com/pod-product-compliance
Lightning Source LLC
Chambersburg PA
CBHW020324200626
46814CB00006BB/2404